"I'm hardly your type, Brand," Cassie said.

"I mean, if you're looking for potential fiancées, you've got plenty of women to choose from."

"Cassie, Cassie." Brand shook his head. Then, in a move that caught her completely unprepared, he reached forward and traced the curve of her cheek with the tip of one finger. The brief touch sent a disturbing tremor running through her.

"Don't!" she told him sharply, shying away from the contact.

There was another long silence. Finally Brand said, "Cassie?"

She lifted her chin slowly, brushing her hair back from her face. "What do you expect me to say? *I do*?"

"I don't think it will be necessary to go that far."

"Just what are we supposed to tell people?" she demanded.

His answer, when it came, unleashed a flood of images in her mind. "We don't tell them. We show them."

Dear Reader:

Happy October! The temperature is crisp, the leaves on the trees are putting on their annual color show and the daylight hours are getting shorter. What better time to cuddle up with a good book? What better time for Silhouette Romance?

And in October, we've got an extraspecial lineup. Continuing our DIAMOND JUBILEE celebration is Stella Bagwell—with *Gentle as a Lamb*. The wolf is at shepherdess Colleen McNair's door until she meets up with Jonas Dobbs—but is he friend or the ultimate foe? Only by trusting her heart can she tell for sure. . . . Don't miss this wonderful tale of love.

The DIAMOND JUBILEE—Silhouette Romance's tenth anniversary celebration—is our way of saying thanks to you, our readers. To symbolize the timelessness of love, as well as the modern gift of the tenth anniversary, we're presenting readers with a DIAMOND JUBILEE Silhouette Romance each month, penned by one of your favorite Silhouette Romance authors. In the coming months, writers such as Lucy Gordon and Phyllis Halldorson are writing DIAMOND JUBILEE titles especially for you.

And that's not all! There are six books a month from Silhouette Romance—stories by wonderful writers who time and time again bring home the magic of love. During our anniversary year, each book is special and written with romance in mind. October brings you *Joey's Father* by Elizabeth August—a heartwarming story with a few surprises in store for the lovely heroine and rugged hero—as well as *Make-believe Marriage*—Carole Buck's debut story in the Silhouette Romance line. *Cimarron Rebel* by Pepper Adams, the third book in the exciting CIMARRON STORIES trilogy, is also coming your way this month! And in the future, work by such loved writers as Diana Palmer, Annette Broadrick and Brittany Young is sure to put a smile on your lips.

During our tenth anniversary, the spirit of celebration is with us year-round. And that's all due to you, our readers. With the support you've given to us, you can look forward to many more years of heartwarming, poignant love stories.

I hope you'll enjoy this book and all of the stories to come. Come home to romance—Silhouette Romance—for always!

Sincerely,

Tara Hughes Gavin
Senior Editor

CAROLE BUCK

Make-believe Marriage

Published by Silhouette Books New York
America's Publisher of Contemporary Romance

SILHOUETTE BOOKS
300 E. 42nd St., New York, N.Y. 10017

ISBN: 0-373-08752-7

First Silhouette Books printing October 1990

Printed in the U.S.A.

Books by Carole Buck

Silhouette Romance

Make-believe Marriage #752

Silhouette Desire

Time Enough For Love #565

CAROLE BUCK

is a television news writer and movie reviewer who lives in Atlanta. She is single. Her hobbies include cake decorating, ballet and traveling. She collects frogs, but does not kiss them. Carole says she's in love with life; she hopes the books she writes reflect this.

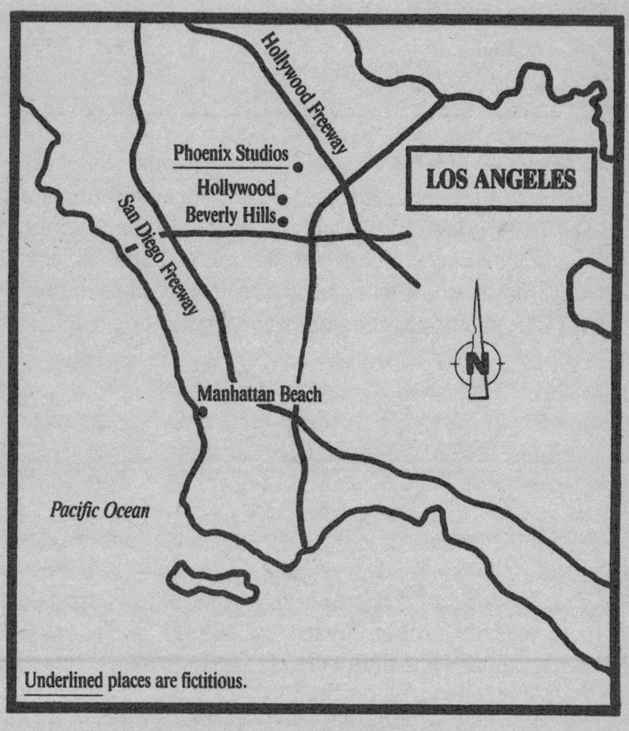
Hollywood Freeway
Phoenix Studios
Hollywood
Beverly Hills
LOS ANGELES
San Diego Freeway
N
Manhattan Beach
Pacific Ocean
Underlined places are fictitious.

Chapter One

Cassandra Leigh Addams had been all of ten days old the first time she'd gone through the impressive front gate of Phoenix Studios in Hollywood. While she had no recollection of the occasion, publicity stills she'd seen later informed her that her behavior had been less than angelic and her appearance less than photogenic.

Phoenix Studios had always been an important part of Cassie's life. It was where her parents—actress Sabrina Leigh and producer Christopher Addams—had found fame, fortune and each other. Even now, nearly twelve years after their deaths in a plane crash, the imprint of their personalities still lingered on the lot.

Cassie had spent countless hours at the studio as a child. She'd used it as her personal playground in many ways, unconsciously absorbing the rudiments and realities of filmmaking even as she retained an innocent delight in movie magic. While she'd had far fewer opportunities to visit the studio during her teens, she'd always made the most of the ones she'd gotten.

Two years before—about the time of her twenty-second birthday—Cassie had come to Phoenix to go to work. Not for the studio exactly. Rather, she'd been hired as a production assistant to Marcus Moviemaking, the production company of Brandon—Brand—Marcus, the gifted young director who had a lucrative multipicture development deal with Phoenix.

The building that housed Marcus Moviemaking was tucked away on a pleasantly landscaped corner of the sprawling Phoenix lot. It was a perfect location except for one thing. Convenient parking spaces were in short supply and Cassie frequently had to hunt for five or ten minutes before she found a place to leave her car. On this particular Monday, however, she lucked into an empty slot less than a hundred yards from the front door of her workplace.

As she maneuvered her car into the narrow space, Cassie once again reviewed her mental checklist of the errands she'd had to run that morning. Roughly six months before, she'd been asked if she wanted to be Brand's personal assistant. She'd waited all of five seconds to say yes. She'd known the job would place her at the very center of the creative process.

She'd also known it would require she regularly perform duties such as carting her boss's clothes to the dry cleaner's and taking his expensive Italian sports car in for tune-ups. She'd been more than willing to fetch and carry. And while she hadn't realized that she'd also be expected to track down sources of the exotic foodstuffs Brand had developed a taste for while filming on location in Bangkok four years before, she'd swiftly familiarized herself with every Thai restaurant in the area.

After assuring herself that she'd completed all the tasks she'd had to do before coming into the office, Cassie turned off the engine of her car. Glancing in the rearview mirror, she assessed herself with critical hazel eyes.

She noted unhappily that there appeared to be a new crop of freckles on her nose. She'd eaten off most of her lip gloss, too. But, heaven knew, her mouth was noticeable enough without having extra attention called to it. As for her hair...

Cassie frowned at her reflection. She did her best to keep her thick red-gold tresses tamed into a no-nonsense braid. Still, there were always untidy wisps and tendrils clinging to her forehead and cheeks. She brushed at the fine strands impatiently. Maybe a quick visit to a salon would help, she thought with a trace of exasperation.

Except there was no such thing as a "quick" visit to a salon in Hollywood, and Cassie well knew it. She could still vividly recall the endless hours her mother had spent with hairdressers, makeup artists, manicurists, dress designers and the like. Once in a very great while, Cassie had been included in these sessions. Unfortunately she'd never developed a taste for the rituals of coiffure, couture and cosmetics. Nor had she enjoyed having her appearance dissected feature by feature. Even now she could hear her mother's dulcet voice cataloging each and every flaw.

Warding off this memory with a quick shake of her head, Cassie abandoned her halfhearted efforts at primping and got out of her slightly battered compact car. The temperature outside was in the upper fifties, a little cooler than usual for Los Angeles at the end of May. She was grateful for the oatmeal-colored cotton sweater she'd layered over her workday outfit of jeans and a man-tailored oxford cloth shirt.

She hefted the strap of her canvas tote-cum-briefcase over her shoulder as she slammed the car door shut. The lock didn't quite catch, so she reopened the door and slammed it a second time.

Cassie's uncle and former legal guardian, Jordan Addams, had been hinting—quite subtly for him—that he was thinking about buying her a sleek and sporty imported automobile as a twenty-fourth birthday gift. She'd told him flat out on at least four different occasions that she was perfectly content with what she was driving.

Cassie knew that her current mode of transportation offended her uncle's status-conscious sensibilities. As one of Hollywood's most powerful agents, Jordan Addams placed great emphasis on image. Perception was reality as far as he was concerned. The idea that *his* niece was blithely tooling around town in a clunker disturbed him.

Cassie was honest enough with herself to admit that her decision to keep driving her seven-year-old compact probably was a form of rebellion against the control her uncle tried to exercise over her life. But at the same time, she genuinely liked the car. It did what it was supposed to do with no muss and no fuss.

Cassie gave the dented spot on the hood of her car an affectionate pat, then turned to head to work. As she did, she was hailed by a familiar voice.

"Hey, Cassie!"

"Lee!" Cassie responded happily. The short curly-haired man approaching her at a brisk march was Lee—short for Leonard—Allen, Marcus Moviemaking's location manager. He was in his early thirties and attractive in an offbeat way. "I was afraid I wasn't going to get a chance to say goodbye before you took off. Brand had so many things for me to do this morning before I came in—"

"He's trying to keep us apart, you know," Lee interrupted, his voice dropping into a mock-conspiratorial tone.

"Oh, sure. That's why he's having me be your liaison while you're in Texas."

"That's professional. I'm talking personal."

"You're talking nonsense, Lee," Cassie returned with a laugh. She and the location manager were friends and that was all. She enjoyed his company and admired his competence, but she wasn't attracted to him. And he certainly wasn't attracted to her. Lee had a weakness for bosomy blondes.

"Nonsense?" Lee looked offended. "He's had it in for me ever since I made that remark about your legs the first time I saw you wearing a skirt."

"What remark about—" Cassie began, then broke off abruptly as she realized what he was referring to. A memory she'd made quite an effort to suppress surfaced. She started to flush. "Oh."

The remark in question had been complimentary in the extreme. Lee had voiced it, none too discreetly, on a crowded and busy set, about a month after she'd accepted the job as Brand Marcus's personal assistant.

Cassie could still remember how startled and embarrassed the comment had made her feel. She'd been even more unsettled by the fact that Brand, who'd overhead the remark, had given Lee a look that could have frozen water at fifty paces.

And then there had been the look her boss had given her. Cassie didn't know how to describe the expression she'd seen in Brand's brilliant blue eyes in that moment, except to say that it had made her cheeks go hot and her knees turn to jelly.

"It's all coming back to you, hmm?" Lee teased.

"Unfortunately, yes," Cassie answered, shifting her shoulder bag. She decided it was time to change the subject. "Ah, so, how are things shaping up in Texas?"

Lee rolled his dark eyes. "Don't ask. Why Brand isn't shooting *Prodigal* here in L.A., I don't know."

Cassie bristled. *Prodigal* was Brand's latest production. The project was one that, since its inception, had meant a great deal to her. Her opinions about how the film should be made were very strong.

"He isn't shooting it in L.A. because *Prodigal* needs to be done on location, Lee," she said. "You can fake the look and feel of a place for some pictures, but not this one."

An odd expression flickered across Lee's face. "How many times did you and Brand rehearse that spiel?"

"Excuse me?"

"The other day when I made my final pitch for finding a California location to double as the Texas panhandle, he used almost the same words to turn me down."

"Oh." Cassie experienced a peculiar tingle of pleasure at this revelation. "Well, we've never really discussed it, but—"

"But you think alike," Lee concluded. "Yeah, I've noticed." He glanced quickly at his wristwatch. "Look, I've got to go. I'll call you tomorrow, Cassie."

"Sure." Cassie nodded. "Have a good trip."

"I'll settle for surviving it. Take care." The location manager started to turn away, then snapped his fingers and turned back. "Oh, one more thing."

"Yes?"

"I'd tiptoe around Brand when you go in. Something's eating at him." Lee grimaced. "Maybe it's the fact that we're seven weeks from the start of principal photography and he hasn't cast the two lead roles yet."

Cassie stiffened. "He knows who he wants, Lee."

"True. But *we* know it's damned unlikely he's going to get them."

Cassie was frowning when she pulled open the heavy glass door of the Marcus Moviemaking's offices a few seconds later.

"Cassie!" This sharp exclamation greeted her the split second she set foot inside the lobby of the building. Its source was a plain middle-aged woman who was standing beside the reception desk, handing something to the doe-eyed blonde sitting behind it. The woman was Noreen Krebs, Brand's office manager. Noreen had begun working for Brand more than ten years before, when he'd come to Phoenix Studios to direct his first made-for-TV movie. She was fierce loyal, ferociously efficient and decidedly tart-tongued.

"Hi, Noreen." Cassie liked the older woman very much and valued her good opinion. She nodded at the receptionist. "Hi, Tina."

"Hi," Tina returned breathily. "Did you see the—"

"He wants you in his office, Cassie," Noreen interrupted. There was no need for her to define who "he" was.

Cassie adjusted the strap of her weighty shoulder bag. "Right now?"

"If not sooner."

"Should I go in waving a white flag?"

"Try wearing body armor."

"Oh, terrific. Have I done something?"

"I'm sure you'll find out."

"Brand wasn't in a very good mood when he came in this morning," Tina volunteered helpfully, wrinkling her pert nose.

"So Lee Allen said," Cassie replied. "I saw him in the parking lot when I was coming in. He thinks Brand is worried about *Prodigal*."

Noreen raised her brows. "There are definitely a few things to be worried about."

Cassie nodded her agreement, then gestured in the direction of Brand's office with a flippancy she was far from feeling. "Well, away I go," she announced. "Remember me kindly if I don't return."

The cream-colored hall that led to her destination was hung with framed posters, all of Marcus Moviemaking's productions. Cassie normally got a jolt of inspiration when she walked by them. Now, however, she barely noticed the impressive display. She was too busy trying to quell a mounting sense of uneasiness.

Try wearing body armor, Noreen Krebs had said. It had sounded like a joke. Unfortunately Cassie had the distinct impression the older woman hadn't been trying to be funny, which probably meant that she, Cassie, had made some sort of mistake.

But what?

Cassie worked hard at her job and she believed she was good at it. While she lacked self-confidence in a number of areas, she had faith in her professional competence. Brand apparently did, too. After all, he'd promoted her to be his personal assistant. What's more, he'd been steadily increasing her responsibilities during the past months.

There were also occasions when, as Lee Allen had suggested a few minutes before, she and Brand seemed linked by some form of mental telepathy. She had a knack for anticipating his needs. He had an uncanny talent for bringing up subjects at the same time she was thinking about them.

Yet Cassie couldn't quite get a fix on where she stood with Brand. There didn't seem to be much consistency in his treatment of her. While she was well aware that creative talent such as his tended to breed a mercurial temperament, she found there was something decidedly unnerving about working for a man who seemed to focus on her to the exclusion of all else one minute, then virtually forget about her the next. Brand was perfectly capable of shifting from charming her to chewing her out and back again in the space of a single conversation—sometimes in the space of a single sentence!

Not, she had to concede, that her on-the-job behavior was the epitome of moderation. She had a temper, and a tendency to speak first and apologize afterward. While she was utterly devoted to her work, she was far from being a dutifully docile employee. Still, she had the feeling her boss preferred it that way.

Dealing closely with Brandon Marcus on a day-to-day basis wasn't easy. Exhilarating, exciting and educational, yes. Easy, no. There were moments when Cassie felt as though she were trying to juggle raw eggs and live porcupines while riding a pogo stick.

The door to Brand's office was ajar, as usual. Cassie squared her slim shoulders and prepared for the worst. She knocked once.

"What?" The tone of this single syllable response was about as welcoming as a barbed-wire fence.

Cassie stuck her head through the opening between the door and the frame. Brand was sitting behind his desk, writing something on a notepad.

"It's Cassie," she announced. "Noreen said—"

"Come in," he interrupted without even glancing at her.

Cassie stepped inside and waited.

Brand tapped the pen he'd been writing with against his desk, then shook his head once, as though he was displeased. He crossed out something on the pad with a ruthless slash of the pen. The sudden, almost savage movement made Cassie focus on his hands. Elegantly shaped, yet obviously strong, they were hands that struck her as being as capable of crushing something as caressing it.

Cassie fiddled with the strap of her bag, growing more uncomfortable with each passing second.

"Close the door," Brand instructed tersely, his eyes still fixed on the page in front of him. "And sit down."

After a brief hesitation, Cassie did as she'd been bidden. She let her shoulder bag slide to the floor with a thud as she seated herself in one of the chrome-and-leather chairs placed in front of Brand's desk. She opened her mouth to say something—anything—then closed it again. Instinct told her that, in this instance, silence was the best policy. Folding her hands in her lap, Cassie gazed wordlessly at her employer, trying to figure out what she'd done wrong.

The silence seemed to last for a long time. Finally Brand put the pad and pen aside. His movements were very deliberate, very precise—as though he was exercising great control over them. After a moment, he looked across the desk at Cassie.

Cassie knew a great many people described Brandon Marcus as "handsome." But she considered that too bland a word to sum up his looks.

At thirty-three, Brand had a lean, sculpted face that was a compelling amalgam of complexities and contradictions. There was arrogance in the jut of his cheekbones and jaw, and the promise of self-deprecating humor in the fine faint lines that radiated from the outer corners of his long-lashed eyes. His brow was that of an austere intellectual. His mouth was that of a hedonistic renegade. The striking sapphire of his irises could snap and sizzle one second, then go hard and arctic cold the next.

At the moment, Brand's eyes held an expression Cassie couldn't interpret. For one crazy instant, she was reminded of the way he'd reacted the time Lee Allen had complimented her legs. Shifting nervously, she averted her gaze for a second. When she looked back, the expression was gone.

"Noreen said you wanted to see me," she said, hoping her voice didn't sound as reedy to Brand as it did to her.

Brand opened the top drawer of his desk and pulled out a tabloid newspaper. He tossed it down on the desk.

"Would you care to explain this?" His tone was quiet, but there was no mistaking the command behind the question. Cassie was going to explain, whether she cared to or not.

Moistening her suddenly dry lips with a quick lick of her tongue, Cassie looked down at the scandal sheet. Her stomach flip-flopped.

The "this" in question was a not very flattering black-and-white photograph of her and Chet Walker, one of Hollywood's hottest young male stars. The two of them were welded together in what appeared to be an intimate embrace.

Cassie groaned, feeling her cheeks heat with a mixture of anger and embarrassment.

"That's all?" Brand inquired after several seconds.

"What?" Cassie looked into his eyes and wished she hadn't.

"That's all you have to say?"

Cassie took considerable exception to his tone. "What do you want me to say?" she demanded. "That it's an awful picture? Fine. It's an awful picture. I realize I don't have a lot of good angles, but this photo was definitely taken from one of my worst. I mean, I look a lot better from the left—"

"Cassie." Brand's voice sliced across her stream of words, cutting off the defensive-sounding babble.

She stared at him, mouth slack. After a second, she pressed her lips shut.

"I don't give a damn about the composition of the photograph," he informed her, raking his fingers back through his thick panther-black hair. "I'm concerned with the content."

"The content?" Cassie repeated, blinking. Then comprehension clobbered her like a rock between the eyes. "Don't tell me you're taking this picture seriously!" Her voice jumped about an octave on the final word.

"You're not?"

"Of course I'm not! For heaven's sake, Brand!" Cassie gestured with both hands as she tried to tidy her disordered thoughts to the point where she could express herself coherently. "You know how the tabloids are. If they can't get the genuine goods on somebody, they make things up. They manufacture stories, manufacture pictures—"

"You're saying this photo is a fake?"

Cassie desperately wished she could say precisely that. Unfortunately she couldn't.

"Well, um, no," she conceded reluctantly, dropping her eyes and her voice. "Not . . . exactly."

"Not exactly?"

"It's not what it looks like," she insisted, realizing she was blushing like a guilty schoolgirl and hating it. She brought her head up again. "I hardly *know* Chet Walker!"

Brand lifted a brow. "He seems to know you rather well."

Cassie clenched her hands into fists, fighting the urge to grab the paper, rip it into shreds and throw the pieces in Brand's face. This was the fourth time in two months he'd questioned her about some published reference to her social life. While she was able to tolerate such inquiries from her uncle, she found them infuriating when they came from her employer. Especially given the fact that he, himself, had been a prime subject of tabloid headlines for years!

Just where did Brandon Marcus, of all people, get the idea that he had the right to go digging into her personal affairs? Not that there were any "affairs" for him to dig into. But even if there had been, what she did when she wasn't working was no business of his! And what *he* did when *he* wasn't working was no business of *hers*! What did she care if he had a string of women stretching from—

Cassie swiftly rerouted the direction of this last thought. Taking a deep breath, she glanced down at the tabloid. She knew it was Chet Walker she should really be angry with. Chet Walker, to say nothing of the photographer who'd snapped the picture. Yet it was Brand who was the lightning rod of her stormy emotions.

"Cassie?"

She raised her hazel eyes once more and glared at him. "Chet Walker used to be one of my uncle's clients. We've met a few times. We happened to run into each other at a premiere party last week."

"And Chet decided to grab a quick grope while giving a demonstration of how to perform mouth-to-mouth resuscitation on you?"

"He's a very...uninhibited...person." Cassie nearly choked on the adjective, but some perverse instinct stopped her from telling Brand exactly how unexpected—and unwelcome—Chet's alcohol-induced advances had been.

"You're aware of the kind of reputation he has."

"Oh, yes," she retorted, goaded beyond good sense. "It's almost as bad as yours."

Something that looked very much like anger flared in the depths of Brand's blue eyes. His features hardened. "All the more reason for you to steer clear of him, don't you think?" he inquired levelly.

Cassie was already regretting what she'd said. It had been unfair. While Brand made no secret of the fact that his lifestyle was less than saintly, she knew he had nothing but contempt for the cesspool of self-indulgence in which Chet and his crowd wallowed.

"Brand, I'm sorry. I shouldn't have said—"

Brand seemed to pull back. "Did it ever occur to you that people might be worried about you?" he asked abruptly.

The question caught Cassie completely by surprise. "Worried?"

"Yes. You've been running with a very fast crowd lately. Your uncle's been concerned."

Cassie stared at Brand in disbelief. "You—" Her voice split on the word. She cleared her throat and started again. "You've got to be joking!"

Because her parents had been celebrities, Cassie had grown up with the children of the rich and famous. She was willing to concede that some of them were pretty wild. And because of her ambitions and the way the movie industry worked, she tended to socialize—when she did socialize—with Hollywood's young movers and shakers. She was willing to concede that some of them were pretty wild, too. But to suggest that she "ran" with a very fast crowd was utterly ridiculous!

Cassie drank very little. She didn't touch drugs. And against all odds, she was still a virgin. Although her lack of sexual experience was partly due to her uncle's overprotectiveness and her own insecurity, it also had a great deal to do with her basic values.

While others were comfortable with the idea of casual sex, of getting close without committing, Cassie wasn't. Someday, she hoped, she would find a man with whom she could share her life and her love, not just her bed and her body.

"No, I'm not joking," Brand assured her, steepling his long, lean fingers. "Your uncle can read, you know. And in case you hadn't noticed, your name has been turning up in the tabloids on a fairly regular basis since you became my assistant."

"Of course, I've noticed!" Cassie snapped. She'd also noticed that her name was about the only thing the scandal press got right. She opened her mouth to tell Brand this, but the same perverse instinct that had made her hold her tongue about Chet Walker made her shut it once again. It was none of Brand's business what she did—or didn't do—in her private life!

"Just how do you happen to be so well-informed about my uncle's concerns about me?" she inquired in a tight voice.

"Because we've spoken about it."

Cassie sat bolt upright. "You've been talking about me behind my back?"

"Yes," Brand replied without a flicker of apology.

"For heaven's sake! I'm not a child!"

"I realize that. But—" Brand paused, appearing to debate what his next words should be "—Jordan still thinks you need looking out for."

Cassie cocked her chin challengingly. "And what do *you* think?"

Brand's azure gaze swept over her. "There are moments when I think he's absolutely right."

Cassie felt as though she'd been slapped. She felt even worse a second later when an appalling possibility occurred to her. No, she thought. It couldn't be. She'd *earned* her job, hadn't she? Brand couldn't have promoted her because—

"Cassie?" Brand asked sharply.

She gripped the arms of the chair. "Did you give me the job as your personal assistant because of some sort of deal with my uncle?" she asked in a rush. Her anger over Brand's queries about the tabloid photo of her and Chet Walker was superseded by a sickening sense of anxiety. What if she'd advanced because of her uncle's pull and protectiveness rather than her own ability? What if her current position was some kind of sham?

The question seemed to startle Brand. After a moment, he shook his head. "No."

"Really?" she demanded.

"You know me better than that, Cassie," Brand responded quietly, his eyes very steady.

"Do I?" she parried. "I didn't have the foggiest idea you have a penchant for discussing my private life with my uncle until just a minute ago! Maybe he asked you to do him a favor and look after me by giving me—"

"I didn't *give* you anything," he interrupted, spitting out the denial as though he found the scenario she'd suggested totally unpalatable. "I offered you the job as my assistant because you were the best candidate around. I don't deny that being Jordan Addams's niece got you an interview when you applied for a production slot two years ago. But it didn't get you hired and it certainly didn't get you promoted."

Cassie remained silent for several seconds. She desperately wanted to believe what Brand had just said. But she couldn't quite bring herself to accept that he was telling her the truth.

"Being Jordan Addams's niece won't keep you from getting the boot, either, if you goof up," Brand added.

Oddly enough, Cassie found this categorical statement reassuring. "It won't?"

"No, it won't," he affirmed, then leaned back in his chair. "Does that make you feel better?"

"Actually, yes," she admitted with a little smile. She didn't mind the amusement she'd heard lurking in his inquiry. After a moment, she grew serious again. "I still don't like the idea of you and my uncle talking about me behind my back. No matter what the two of you may think, I'm perfectly capable of taking care of myself."

Brand's gaze moved deliberately from Cassie's face to the tabloid and back again. He didn't say a word. He didn't need to.

Cassie bit back a singularly unladylike expression. "Next time I'll knee him in the groin, all right?" she asked in an exasperated tone.

"From what I've heard, Chet would probably enjoy that" came the cynical retort. Before Cassie had a chance to respond, Brand rose to his feet, coming to his full six-foot height in one lithe movement. "Enough of this," he declared abruptly. "I've got business to take care of and so do you."

"But—"

Ignoring her effort to shoehorn in an objection, Brand proceeded to reel off a series of things he wanted her to do. "Got it?" he said in conclusion.

Cassie was on her feet by this time, too, clamping down on a surge of anger at his unilateral change of subjects. She had no other option—not if she wanted to keep her job. One of the first things she'd learned at Marcus Moviemaking was that when Brandon Marcus decided to shift gears and move ahead, the people he employed either got on board, got out of the way or got run over.

"Got it," she said, matching his tone.

"Fine." Brand stretched, catlike, as though trying to rid his body of tension. The movement pulled the fabric of the black jersey he was wearing taut. Cassie saw the subtle rippling of the muscles of his chest and shoulders beneath the knit material.

"Is that all?" she asked, aware of a curious fluttering in her stomach. Cassie chalked it up to nerves.

"For now." Brand paused for a second, then indicated the tabloid still sitting on his desk with a brief nod. "Do you want that?"

"No, thank you," Cassie refused tartly, bending over to retrieve her shoulder bag. She straightened, flipping her thick plait of hair back behind her shoulder with a quick toss of her head. "I'm not planning to line the bottoms of any bird cages."

Brand said nothing, but one corner of his mouth quirked upward.

"Anything else?" Cassie asked, tugging down on the front of her sweater.

"No," he replied with a shake of his head. "But I know how to whistle if there is."

"How to— Oh." Cassie felt herself color as she realized he was harking back to something she'd said at her interview six months before.

Her memory replayed the episode in mortifying detail.

She'd floated toward the door, giddy with a sense of personal accomplishment. As she'd put her hand on the knob, she'd suddenly taken note of one of the pieces of artwork on the office wall. Brand had a remarkable collection of vintage movie posters from the thirties and forties. The one she'd focused on happened to advertise the 1944 Humphrey Bogart-Lauren Bacall film, *To Have and Have Not*.

Cassie still couldn't explain why she'd surrendered to the impulse that had hit her the instant she'd seen the poster. Instead of making a quiet, dignified exit, she'd turned back to Brand and struck a theatrical pose. She'd then quoted Bacall's famous lines instructing Bogart on how he should whistle if he wanted her.

"I was hoping you'd forgotten about that," she told Brand with a grimace of embarrassment.

"That's hardly likely. You made quite an impression."

"I can't imagine what you must have thought."

Brand studied her from beneath partially lowered eyelids, his expression enigmatic. "Probably not," he agreed quietly.

Chapter Two

Three days later, Cassie stood at one end of the bustling Phoenix Studio commissary searching for Noreen Krebs. Clutching a cafeteria tray laden with the meal she'd just purchased, she scanned the crowded dining hall methodically. She finally spotted Noreen at a table about twenty yards away. The older woman was munching on a hamburger and reading a magazine.

"Sorry I'm late," Cassie apologized once she'd threaded her way through the lunch-hour throng. "I got tied up on the phone." She plunked her tray down and slid into the seat opposite Noreen.

"Don't worry about it, Cassie," Noreen responded, putting aside the magazine. "I'm afraid I did go ahead and start eating without you, though."

"No problem," Cassie said, spreading a paper napkin in her lap. She shoved an errant lock of hair back behind her right ear with a quick sweep of her fingers. She'd been too rushed to bother with braiding that morning, so she'd simply bunched her hair up, pinned it into a haphazard knot at the back of her head and hoped for the best. "What were you reading? It looked like you were fascinated."

Noreen picked up the magazine and extended it to Cassie. "An advance copy of this month's *CLOSE-UP*. Brand's the cover story."

Cassie took the glossy publication and studied the front of it. In keeping with *CLOSE-UP*'s style, the cover photograph of Brand was a tightly cropped head shot. It had an unposed, "unauthorized" look. Brand's thick night-black hair was slightly mussed, curling over his collar and around his ears. His vivid blue eyes blazed with intensity. One of his dark brows was quirked upward, lending a hint of sardonic inquiry to his expression. He was smiling at someone—or something—beyond the camera.

The lower right-hand corner of the cover bore the italicized words: *The Marcus Magic*.

After a few seconds, Cassie flipped the magazine open. She leafed slowly through the pages until she came to the article about Brand.

"It's the usual," Noreen observed offhandedly. "All about how Brand was abandoned as a child. How he eventually got placed with a foster father who loved taking home movies. And how he came to Hollywood when he was twenty-two, after winning a national student filmmaking award. You know the drill, Cassie. You've read it dozens of times."

"There's the usual bunch of photographs of Brand and various gorgeous women, I see," Cassie commented after a few seconds, experiencing an unpleasant tightening in her throat.

"Check out the one of him and Sheila Parker."

"I don't see—" Cassie began, then turned the page and felt her heart sink. She made a small involuntary sound of dismay.

"Exactly," Noreen responded dryly.

"Why did they have to print this *now*?"

"It's an absolutely fabulous picture, for one thing."

Cassie sighed and stared at the photograph. She couldn't quarrel with Noreen's hyperbolic description. It *was* an absolutely fabulous picture.

Brand—dark and dashing in the black-and-white severity of a tuxedo.

Sheila—blond and beautiful in a glittering confection of beads and chiffon.

They were magnetic individuals and they made an extraordinarily compelling couple.

Cassie slapped the magazine shut and shoved it back across the table at Noreen. "Ancient history," she declared flatly.

"Barely two years ago," Noreen countered. "Right about the time you came to work for Marcus Moviemaking."

Cassie wished she could blot the image of Brand and Sheila out of her mind, but she couldn't. The way the two of them had been looking at each other was indelibly etched in her mind.

Cassie had no firsthand knowledge about the affair between Brand and Sheila Parker. According to gossip, it had been a transitory but very torrid fling, which—surprisingly—had ended in an amiable parting rather than some kind of emotional explosion. She knew for a fact that the two were still in touch with each other.

Cassie picked up her fork and began stabbing at the oriental chicken salad she'd ordered for lunch. Although she'd been ravenous when she'd come into the commissary, she no longer felt very hungry.

"I don't imagine Graham Wyatt's going to be too pleased when he sees that photo," Noreen commented with characteristic understatement. "No man likes having his wife's past thrown up in his face."

"He'll never agree to do *Prodigal* after this," Cassie predicted gloomily, chasing a water chestnut around her plate. "And if he says no, Sheila will, too."

Like many people, Cassie had been intrigued by the whirlwind courtship that had culminated in the wedding of

Sheila Parker to Graham Wyatt. The tabloids had had a field day tracking down—or making up—juicy tidbits about the relationship between the beautiful blond actress and the movie idol twenty years her senior.

Now the popular press was claiming that Graham and Sheila's less-than-a-year-old marriage was in trouble. Cassie was inclined to doubt such reports. According to the tabloids, *every* couple in Hollywood was coming asunder. Her own parents had been reported to be on the verge of splitting up at least a dozen times.

Those reports had been complete fabrications. Sabrina Leigh and Christopher Addams had been utterly devoted to each other. Their mutual passion had been so complete, so consuming, that Cassie had felt excluded from the magic circle of their love.

Still, while the scandalmongers had been absolutely wrong about her parents, Cassie had to acknowledge that it was possible they might, just might, be on the trail of the truth where Graham Wyatt and Sheila Parker were concerned. But whether they were or not, there was no doubting that word of Brand's desire to cast the couple in *Prodigal* had added a sensational fillip to the speculation about an impending separation and divorce.

Cassie dropped her fork into the salad bowl, her appetite totally gone.

"Cassie?" Noreen questioned, frowning.

Cassie looked across the table. "Graham Wyatt and Sheila Parker are perfect for this project!" she burst out. "I hate the idea that they're probably going to pass on it."

"Well, if they do pass on it, it will be their loss," Noreen returned. "Some of the hottest actors in town are ready to kill for a chance to play Dan Farlow. And I won't even mention what one Oscar-winning actress said *she's* willing to do just to get a reading for the part of Sally Harper."

Under normal circumstances, Cassie probably would have laughed at the half disbelieving, half disdainful way Noreen delivered the last sentence. Instead, she shook her head in frustration.

"I know all that," she said. "But Graham and Sheila—Oh, don't you see, Noreen? *Prodigal* has so much potential! And if it's done the way it should be done, it'll be a classic. You've read the script. You know what I mean!" Cassie paused, suddenly focusing on the older woman's expression. "What's so funny?" she asked stiffly.

"I'm sorry," Noreen replied, obviously trying to control the smile that was tugging at the corners of her thin-lipped mouth. She sounded more amused than apologetic. "I was just thinking what a perfect pair you and Brand make."

Cassie felt a wave of hot blood surge up her throat and into her face. Had Noreen lost her mind? she wondered. She and Brand—a pair? Good Lord, the women who paraded in and out of Brandon Marcus's life were all accomplished beauties and experienced charmers. And while "accomplished" was a designation Cassie certainly aspired to, she seriously doubted she'd ever be considered a contender in the "beauty" or "charmer" category. As for meriting the adjective *experienced*...

"You were thinking *what*?" she finally managed to choke out.

Noreen stopped smiling and regarded Cassie in a peculiar manner. She remained silent for several seconds, as though weighing her response before making it. The combination of the scrutiny and the silence made Cassie very uncomfortable.

"I only meant that hearing you talk about *Prodigal* is like listening to Brand," Noreen explained slowly. She seemed to test each word before saying it aloud.

"Oh." Cassie found herself shying from the way the older woman seemed bent on bracketing her and Brand together. She hadn't minded when Lee Allen had done the same thing the day before. In fact, she'd been rather pleased. But Noreen seemed to be suggesting something... deeper.

"You know," Noreen went on thoughtfully, an odd look ghosting across her unprepossessing face, "I've often wondered just how far Brand would go to make sure a movie got done the way he believes it should be. I've worked for him for more than a decade now, and I *still* haven't figured out where he'd draw the line."

Noreen's words reverberated in Cassie's head nearly two hours later as she sat at her desk, reading the latest rewrite of the *Prodigal* script.

How far *would* Brand go for this film? she asked herself, twisting a lock of hair around her finger.

And... how far would *I* go?

Prodigal was based on an obscure novel Cassie had picked up by chance several years before. It told the wryly funny, yet deeply touching tale of Dan Farlow, a burned-out big-city cop who finds a reason to live and a woman named Sally Harper to love in a small town in the Texas panhandle.

Cassie had sensed the story's cinematic possibilities from the first. Shortly after starting at Marcus Moviemaking, she'd worked up her nerve and called the book to Brand's attention. He'd been in the middle of editing a film at the time, so she hadn't really expected much of a response.

Cassie had been flabbergasted when Brand had read the novel and purchased the film rights within the space of a week. A little more than a month after that, he'd stunned her speechless by asking her to take a look at the first draft of the screen adaptation he'd written.

Cassie had stayed up all night reading and rereading the script. It had been brilliant.

As often happened, copies of the *Prodigal* script had begun circulating around the industry. The "buzz" was positive in terms of artistic merit, but there had been questions about the project's commercial appeal. Cassie knew Brand had been pressured to make changes in the story line and characters. She also knew he'd refused to compromise his vision of the film.

It had taken a year to arrange financing for the picture. And it had been during a protracted negotiating session with a team of industry money men that Cassie had first heard Brand suggest Graham Wyatt and Sheila Parker for the title roles.

Her initial reaction to the idea had been negative. She hadn't been able to imagine the actor whose suave, sophisticated performances had made him a superstar as the down-and-out Dan. Nor could she see the unquestionably gifted but oh-so-glamorous Sheila Parker playing the part of the plain and practical Sally.

Then Cassie had rented videotapes of several of Graham Wyatt's lesser-known films. She'd viewed them at home and realized that the polished leading man was capable of shedding his star persona and transforming himself into a variety of offbeat characters. She'd also remembered that Sheila Parker had made a wrenchingly effective screen debut in the role of a mousy, battered wife.

Suddenly Brand's casting idea had begun to seem as inspired as it was unorthodox.

Cassie sighed as she studied the dialogue revisions for one of the film's most pivotal exchanges. She was now at the point where she could *hear* Graham Wyatt and Sheila Parker saying these words. She could *see* them playing this scene. They were Dan and Sally as far as she was concerned.

The thought of their refusing to do *Prodigal* was almost unendurable.

So was the thought that there was nothing she could do to influence their decision.

There was an abrupt knock at her door. Before Cassie had a chance to respond, the door swung open to reveal Brand. He stood still and silent for several seconds. His tall, whipcord-lean body radiated a palpable aura of aggressive energy. His eyes were hidden behind mirror-lensed sunglasses.

"Brand!" Cassie exclaimed, genuinely startled. It had been months since her boss had so much as stuck his nose into the cluttered cubbyhole she'd been assigned after her promotion. Her broom-closet-sized work space was located down the hall from his spacious office. When he wanted her, which was about ten or fifteen times a day, he either buzzed her on the intercom system or yelled.

"I need you in my office," he said without preamble.

"But—" She stood, shoving a stray piece of hair back behind her ear and fervently wishing that she hadn't succumbed to her in-office habit of kicking off her shoes when she'd returned to her desk after lunch.

"Now, Cassie. It's important." With that, Brand pivoted on one heel and headed down the hall.

Cassie was galvanized into action by his last word. She paused just long enough to locate and slip on her shoes, then followed Brand. He neither slowed his pace to allow her to catch up nor glanced back to make sure she was complying with his order.

Surprisingly Brand did pause outside his office and allow her to enter first. Cassie moved by him with an escalating sense of uneasiness. The sound of the door shutting behind her did nothing to reduce her anxiety level.

"Sit down," Brand instructed, crossing to his desk. He unzipped the bombadier-style leather jacket he had on, then shrugged the expensive garment off with a smooth movement and carelessly tossed it aside. "Please," he added quietly.

This courtesy unnerved Cassie more than anything else. She did as requested, gingerly seating herself in the same chair she'd occupied three days before. Her pulse was racing.

Brand perched himself on the edge of his desk, forking one hand back though his hair. The sunlight pouring in from the window behind him threw his virile profile into strong relief. After a few moments, he pulled off his sunglasses and dropped them onto the desk. His sapphire gaze swept over Cassie like a wave, assessing her from top to toe.

"Did you get the latest revisions on *Prodigal*?" he asked after a few moments.

Cassie was taken aback by this opening conversational gambit. She nodded warily.

"And?" Brand prompted.

"And they're terrific. Especially the new scene at the church supper." She swatted a lock of hair away from her cheek. "But you don't need me to tell you what a good screenwriter you are."

One corner of Brand's mouth curled upward. "Oh, I don't know about that," he commented reflectively. "It's always nice to have my high opinion of my talents confirmed by someone else."

Cassie grimaced. She'd accused Brand of arrogance on more than one occasion. "I didn't mean it that way," she muttered, looking down. What was going on? she wondered. She didn't believe for a moment that she'd been summoned in here to engage in polite chitchat about the *Prodigal* script. Why didn't Brand get to the point?

"You didn't?"

Cassie looked up. "No, I didn't," she replied, feeling more and more unsettled by her employer's behavior. "Oh, for heaven's sake, Brand! You've probably had a dozen people read the revisions and rave over them. What I think is superfluous."

There was a moment or two of silence.

Brand rubbed his chin with one hand. There was a faint shadowing of late-afternoon beard growth on his jaw.

"If you honestly believe that, Cassie," he said finally, "we've got a serious problem." He spoke very softly, more to himself than to her.

Cassie was completely confused now. She didn't know what to make of his tone. His expression was equally difficult to decipher. "I don't understand," she admitted.

Brand's lips thinned and his eyes darkened. "No, I don't suppose you do."

His words stung. Cassie didn't know what kind of game Brand was playing, but she was sick of it. "Look, will you please tell me why you dragged me in here?" she demanded.

"I just had a meeting with Aaron Chase."

Cassie caught her breath. Like her uncle, Aaron Chase was an agent. His client list included both Graham Wyatt and Sheila Parker.

"What did he say?" she asked, leaning forward.

"Graham and Sheila have read the *Prodigal* script. They both love it."

"But?" She felt as though she were trying to pry open a clam that had been cemented shut.

"But they have reservations about the project."

Cassie abruptly decided it was time for one of the participants in this discussion to be direct. Since Brand apparently wasn't going to do the honors, it was left to her to uphold the cause of candor.

"Reservations stemming from the fact that you had an affair with Sheila," she summed up bluntly.

"Yes." The affirmation was flat and cool. So was the expression in his eyes. "The bottom line is that Graham wants the part I wrote, but he doesn't want any part of me. He *especially* doesn't want any part of me near his wife."

"Aaron Chase told you that?"

"More or less."

Something unpleasant twisted in the pit of Cassie's stomach. "In other words, Graham Wyatt is jealous of you."

She hadn't meant this assertion to be an accusation. But somehow that's how it came out sounding. She saw Brand's sculpted features harden.

"Graham Wyatt is fifty-four and he's married to a very beautiful woman who's two decades younger than he is," he replied. "I would imagine he's jealous of a great many people." He held Cassie's gaze for a moment, then looked away.

Cassie slumped in her chair, feeling a little sick. "So," she said, carefully keeping her voice steady, "what you're trying to say is, Graham and Sheila aren't going to do the picture. Right?"

There was a short, sharp pause.

"Not necessarily," Brand answered finally. His face was still averted. What Cassie could see of his expression told her about as much as an unengraved tombstone.

"Not necessarily?"

"We may still be able to cast Graham and Sheila."

"How?" Cassie immediately wanted to know. She felt a brief flash of hope. Then an awful thought occurred to her. "Oh, no, Brand! You're not thinking about giving up directing the picture!"

Brand shook his head decisively. "No. Absolutely not."

"Then what are you—" The question Cassie was about to ask caught at the top of her throat as Brand's eyes swung back to meet hers.

"You're the key, Cassie," Brand told her.

"Me?"

"Yes, you. You care about *Prodigal* as much as I do. Maybe more in some ways. You want to see it done the way it should be done. And that means with Graham Wyatt playing Dan Farlow, and Sheila Parker playing Sally Harper."

"But if Graham's jealous of you—"

"If Graham's jealous of me, he and Sheila won't do the film. But if he can be persuaded that there's no reason for him to be jealous, they will. That's where you come in."

No, Cassie thought with a trace of alarm. This is where I go out and tell Noreen that the man we work for has gone bonkers.

"What are you trying to say, Brand?" she asked cautiously.

Even in the most trying of circumstances, Brandon Marcus's sense of dramatic timing was impeccable. He waited one beat . . . two beats. . . .

Then he simply announced, "You and I are going to get engaged."

Chapter Three

Engaged to do what?"

Brand's lips curved into a sardonic approximation of a smile. "Oh, the usual thing," he replied. "Temporarily, of course."

"Of course," Cassie echoed a trifle snidely. Her thoughts had scattered like dry leaves in a hurricane. She scrambled to rake them into some kind of order.

Engaged? Was Brand crazy?

"Is this a joke?" she finally asked.

An emotion she couldn't identify flared deep in Brand's eyes, then disappeared. "No, Cassie," he answered levelly, "it's not a joke."

"You're serious?"

"I'm very serious." Brand leaned toward her, his expression intent. His eyes locked on to hers.

Cassie felt a strange sensation skitter along her nerve endings. She'd seen Brand turn this look, this concentrated manner, on other people. She'd also seen the results he got by doing so. Brandon Marcus had an innate ability to get what he wanted, when he wanted, from whomever he wanted.

"Cassie, look," he began, his voice low and reasonable. "We've agreed that Graham and Sheila are the best choices for the leads in *Prodigal*, right?"

Cassie swallowed. "Right," she conceded carefully.

"Okay, then. Graham Wyatt, the actor, wants to do the part of Dan Farlow because he knows it's the role of a lifetime. The problem is Graham Wyatt, the man. The husband. He *doesn't* want to play the part of Dan Farlow—to work with me—because he's afraid it might endanger his marriage."

"What about his . . . wife?"

"What Sheila does depends entirely on Graham."

"How do you know?"

Brand's expression hardened slightly. "She told me."

There was a short, not very pleasant pause.

Cassie worried her lower lip with her teeth as she tried to sort out the implications of the bizarre scheme Brand was suggesting. "So," she said slowly, "you think that our pretending to get engaged—"

"Graham Wyatt has to be convinced that he's wrong to be afraid for his marriage," Brand interrupted. "That he's wrong to be jealous of me. He has to be made to believe that, despite what happened between us in the past, my interest in Sheila, today, is purely professional. The only way to do both those things is to show him that all my *personal* interest is centered on somebody else."

"And you're proposing—" Cassie broke off abruptly, mentally groaning at her choice of words. "I'm supposed to be this 'somebody else.'"

"Yes."

"But why me?" Cassie's mind flashed back to the magazine article she'd skimmed earlier in the studio commissary. "I'm hardly your type, Brand. I mean, if you're looking for potential fiancées, why don't you pick somebody from the latest issue of *CLOSE-UP*? There's a two-page spread of likely candidates in it. You'll have to exclude Sheila Parker, of course. But aside from that, you've got plenty of women to choose from."

"Cassie, Cassie." Brand shook his head. A comma of dark hair fell down onto his forehead. He brushed it back with an unthinking gesture. Then in a move that caught Cassie completely unprepared, he reached forward and traced the curve of her cheek with the tip of one finger.

The brief touch sent a disturbing tremor running through Cassie. It arrowed along her nervous system like a surge of electricity.

"Don't!" she told him sharply, shying away from the contact.

Brand withdrew his hand, his expression disciplined into unreadability. The blue of his eyes chilled to the color of tempered steel.

"I know what I'm asking of you," he said after a moment. "If I thought there was another way, I'd try it. Believe me. But I don't think there is. As for your question, why you. First of all, because you care about *Prodigal*. Second, because you're the only woman I know I can trust to carry this off."

Cassie dipped her head, suddenly unwilling—or unable—to sustain Brand's potent, probing gaze. She was uncertain how to respond to what he'd just told her.

There was yet another silence. This one lasted longer than the previous ones.

"Cassie?" Brand questioned finally.

She lifted her chin slowly, brushing her hair back from her face. "What do you expect me to say?" she countered with a trace of asperity. "I do?"

"I don't think it will be necessary to go that far."

Cassie shifted in her seat. She crossed and uncrossed her legs. She shifted again. "Do you honestly believe this plan of yours will work?" she asked at last.

"I honestly believe it's worth a try."

"But it's such a crazy idea!"

"Crazy ideas have been known to succeed," Brand told her evenly. "Especially in our business."

Cassie wondered if he'd chosen the word "our" deliberately. Probably. Brandon Marcus was not a man who used language carelessly. She suspected he meant to underscore the professional ties that bound them—and perhaps to flatter her a little by implying that they were equals in this enterprise.

"Just what are we supposed to tell people?" she demanded, unwilling to allow herself to be manipulated so easily.

"As little as possible."

Cassie blinked, taken aback by his answer. "What's that supposed to mean?"

"We don't tell them. We show them."

His last three words unleashed a flood of explicit images in Cassie's mind. She flushed hotly and glanced away. How could she even think about such things?

"You find the scenario so unlikely, Cassie?" Brand questioned quietly after several moments.

Gray-green eyes slewed back to meet crystalline blue ones. "The...scenario?" she repeated, trembling a little. She felt as transparent as glass.

"The two of us," he clarified. "You find it so unlikely?"

She folded her arms across her chest, creating a barrier. "Don't you?"

Brand drummed his fingers against his thighs, watching her intently. "We've been very close the past six months."

"We've been *working*!"

"We've spent more time together than a lot of husbands and wives in this town. You and I know exactly what we have—and haven't—been doing during that time. But no one else does. Not for certain."

"In other words, you want people to think I've been your—that we're—" She couldn't say it. She just couldn't say it.

"It's not a matter of what I want, Cassie," he returned with a hint of heat. "In any case, there are at least a few people who think we've had something going for months."

"What?" The syllable left her lips on a shattered breath. "I don't believe you! I've never heard anything!"

"I'm not surprised. You seem to have a talent for remaining oblivious to the obvious in some situations."

The comment sliced through Cassie like a scalpel, but she forced herself to ignore the hurt. "P-people have said things to you?" she asked raggedly. "Things . . . about us?"

Brand drew a deep breath, then expelled it slowly. She had the feeling he regretted his previous remark. "Yes," he confirmed.

"Who?"

No response. Not even a flicker in his eyes to indicate he'd heard the question.

"Who?" she repeated fiercely.

Brand remained silent for a second longer, then said, "Your uncle, for one."

"Uncle Jordan thinks you and I are lovers?" Shock turned Cassie's voice shrill.

"Not . . . at the moment."

"What does *that* mean?"

For a few moments it seemed as though Brand was going to refuse to reply. Then finally he spoke. His answer was bluntly, bludgeoningly, to the point.

"It means that about a month after you became my assistant, your uncle got wind of a rumor that we were sleeping together," he told her. "He paid me a visit and raised holy hell about it."

Cassie nearly choked. She didn't doubt for an instant that Brand was telling her the truth. While her uncle and onetime legal guardian was a bachelor with a legendary eye for the ladies, he'd always been very old-fashioned where she was concerned. Instead of mellowing as she'd matured, he'd become increasingly Victorian in his attitudes.

"I denied the rumor, of course," Brand went on calmly. "And I told him any intentions I might have toward you were strictly honorable."

Cassie barely registered his final sentence. She was too busy trying not to envision what the meeting between her uncle and her employer must have been like. Unfortunately her fertile imagination refused to cooperate with her efforts to shut it off. It provided a series of painfully vivid and embarrassingly plausible vignettes.

"My uncle believed what you said?" she asked, cheeks burning.

"About our not being lovers?"

She nodded.

Brand's mouth twisted. "I think he would have done his damnedest to take you out of my orbit if he hadn't."

Based on past manifestations of her uncle's overprotective tendencies, Cassie had to agree with this assessment.

"Did you . . . did you tell him anything else?" she questioned uneasily. "About us, I mean. Not—not that there's anything to tell . . ." Her voice trailed off.

"I reminded him that I have a rule about keeping my personal and professional lives separate."

Cassie fiddled with a strand of hair, her mind going around and around like a puppy chasing its tail. Brand did, indeed, have a reputation for refusing to mix business with pleasure. Which, now that she considered it, made her wonder about his earlier statement that some people believed he and she were having an affair. It also made her wonder how he could possibly think that the scheme he'd proposed would ever work.

"Well, then, how are you going to explain our getting engaged?" she challenged. "Wouldn't your 'rule' make it impossible—"

"A man breaks rules when he falls in love, Cassie."

It shocked her to hear Brand speak of love. Just hearing him say the word seemed to underscore the truly appalling nature of the deception he was suggesting.

Cassie clenched her hands into fists, feeling her nails dig into the tender flesh of her palms. "You've really plotted all this out, haven't you, Brand?" The question was far more accusatory than admiring.

"Yes, I have," he acknowledged, apparently unruffled by her tone. "I want *Prodigal* to be the best film it can be, Cassie. I'm not going to leave anything to chance if I can help it."

"And you don't think asking me to pretend to be your fiancée is chancy?"

"No, I don't."

Cassie saw Brand's jaw fret suddenly, and realized he was keeping a very tight rein on himself. For reasons she couldn't adequately explain—and didn't particularly want to explore—it was comforting to her to know that he wasn't as sanguine about the arrangement he was outlining as he was trying to appear.

"Look," he finally continued, "I'm not suggesting we call *Variety*, or the *Hollywood Reporter*, or *CLOSE-UP* magazine tomorrow and announce our engagement. We've got seven weeks before principal photography starts on *Prodigal*. That should give us more than enough time to convince Graham Wyatt and everybody else that we're an item."

"And if it's not?" She cringed inwardly, contemplating the potential for disaster.

"If we get to within three weeks of the start date and I don't have Graham's name on a contract, we'll look at the alternatives."

Cassie remained quiet for several moments, knitting her fingers together, then unraveling them. "You said something about convincing everybody else?" she questioned at last.

Brand's eyes narrowed. *"Everybody,"* he confirmed, underscoring the all-encompassing nature of the word by the emphatic way in which he pronounced it. "Our relationship has to seem absolutely real, Cassie, or this plan won't work. And that means no one but you and I can know the truth."

He glanced down for the space of a few heartbeats, toying with the sunglasses he'd taken off at the beginning of this highly unusual conversation. Eventually he lifted his head and slanted her a searching look.

"Is there someone this charade will cause you problems with?" he asked.

"There are dozens of people!" Cassie retorted, trying to grapple with the enormity of what she was allowing herself to be maneuvered into doing. Deceiving Graham Wyatt for the sake of *Prodigal* was one thing. Not a very nice thing, to be sure. Yet it was something she supposed she could justify if she tried. But what about deceiving her friends and co-workers? How in the world could she justify lying to them?

And good Lord, what about deceiving her Uncle Jordan? If he'd raised holy hell because of an uncomfirmed rumor about her and Brand sleeping together, she shuddered to think of what his reaction to this was going to be!

"No." Brand made a gesture of negation. "What I meant was, is there someone specific—someone special—in your life who might have trouble understanding when this is all over?"

Cassie's cheeks went pink. She shook her head quickly, her fiery hair rippling with the movement.

"Good." Brand nodded. "That makes things easier."

Easier for whom? she wondered.

There was another break in the conversation. Brand seemed to retreat into his thoughts. Cassie tugged restlessly at the bottom of her baggy pullover sweater and squirmed in her seat, trying to sort out her tangled emotions.

It was insane. The whole scheme was utterly and absolutely insane.

"It's not going to work," she muttered.

"What isn't going to work?" Brand asked.

"This pretense! I don't care *what* you say some people think is going on between us, Brand. The idea that you'd want to marry me, or I'd want to marry you, is—is—" Cassie gestured. "No one in his right mind will ever believe it!"

"And how many people in Hollywood do you know who are in their right minds?"

Cassie spent several seconds searching for a suitably quelling comeback. Unfortunately none occurred to her.

"Can't think of anyone?"

She glared at him. "What about Noreen?"

Brand lifted his brows. "Noreen? Mmm. You're right, of course. She's the one exception. Noreen Krebs is definitely in her right mind."

"Well, then?"

"She's also a romantic."

"A romantic?" Cassie couldn't hide her disbelief. "Noreen?"

Brand nodded, the corners of his mouth curling. "Underneath that hard-boiled exterior is a woman who sobs into a lace-trimmed hankie when she watches movies with weddings in them. She'll probably be irritated to think that you and I have been involved and she didn't know it, but she won't be a problem."

Cassie mulled this over. Even if what Brand said about Noreen was true—and she had a hard time accepting that it was—there were many, many other people to consider. Some of them *would* be problems. It was inevitable.

She shook her head. "No."

"No—what?"

She shook her head again. "It won't work."

"It has to."

"Brand—"

"Cassie, this is the only way. Please."

He wasn't pleading with her. Pleading wasn't Brandon Marcus's style. But he was closer to it than Cassie had ever expected—or, in truth, had ever wanted—to hear. She stared at him silently for nearly thirty seconds.

"You're seriously asking me to pretend we're... involved." She retreated into euphemism at the last instant.

"Yes."

"Without telling anyone what I'm—what we're—really doing."

"Exactly."

"All for the sake of a movie."

"For *Prodigal*."

Cassie closed her eyes for a moment. She'd wondered how far Brand would go for a project he believed in. Now she knew. She'd wondered how far she'd go, as well. It appeared she was about to find out.

"Cassie?" Brand prompted softly.

She opened her eyes. "What about afterward?"

"Afterward?"

"Yes. Afterward. After we've wrapped the picture. After there stops being a need for us to pretend we're in love and planning to get married. Have you plotted out who dumps whom? Or are you planning to take ads in the trades announcing it was all a joke?"

Brand stayed silent for several seconds. "I think between the two of us we should be able to script a convincing breakup," he finally stated, his voice tight. "So. Yes or no?"

Cassie was on the edge and she knew she was going to go off. Looking straight at Brand, she took the plunge. "Yes" was all she said.

"You're sure?"

Cassie almost laughed at the absurdity of this question. Was she sure? No, she wasn't sure. In fact, she'd never been less sure about anything in her life!

"Yes," she repeated through gritted teeth.

Brand waited a moment, then nodded. "Good."

Cassie surreptitiously wiped her palms on her slacks. She felt a little woozy. "So what do we do now?"

"I've been invited to a birthday party tonight," he said, giving no indication he'd noticed her distress. He then mentioned the name of an extremely well-known producer and an equally famous restaurant. "I thought we could make our debut as a couple there."

Cassie winced. The party Brand wanted them to attend was an A-list social event.

"Couldn't we have a—sneak preview first?" she suggested. "I mean, wouldn't it make more sense to try out our, ah, act in front of a slightly smaller audience?"

For a moment, Brand seemed on the verge of reaching out to touch her again. She saw him shift his weight, then go still. There was a quality of resistance to his immobility, as though he was fighting a very powerful physical impulse.

"We don't have time for that, Cassie," he said after a few seconds. "I'm sorry."

He sounded sincere. Cassie sighed and reluctantly nodded her understanding. "That's show biz, right?" she returned, trying for a casual tone.

"Something like that." Brand levered himself off his desk. His manner became very businesslike. "I'll pick you up at your place at say, hmm, eight o'clock."

Cassie nodded her agreement, then stood slowly. Doubts assailed her from all directions. "Brand, I'm not much of an actress, you know," she warned. Even to her own ears, her voice sounded very frayed around the edges.

"You don't have to be," he responded steadily. "Just take your cues from me."

Somehow Cassie didn't find this a very comforting notion.

"There is . . . one thing," she said after a few moments.

"Yes?"

Cassie's stomach knotted. There was no delicate way to phrase the question she knew she had to ask—the question she *should* have asked as soon as Brand had put forward his plan. And there was no adequate explanation for why she hadn't asked it before this. Except, perhaps, that she was afraid of what the answer might be.

"Cassie?"

"Is there any reason for Graham Wyatt to be jealous of you?" she demanded bluntly. "Aside from what happened between you and Sheila in the past, I mean. Because if there is—if you and she are still involved—I won't be a party to this, Brand. Not even for *Prodigal*. I mean it. I won't."

Every trace of expression disappeared from Brand's face. It was like watching a blackboard being wiped clean by an invisible hand.

"Sheila and I are friends," he said. "We were lovers once, but now we're friends." He paused briefly, then asked, "Do you have a problem with that?"

Cassie hesitated, then shook her head.

"Fine." It was clear Brand was slamming the door on the topic. "Is there anything else?"

There was a lot else. But instinct told Cassie that this was not the time to bring any of it up. She had more on her plate than she could digest as it was. "No. Nothing else."

Brand nodded, everything in his manner communicating dismissal. "Tonight at eight, then."

"Tonight at eight," she affirmed automatically, then turned to leave. She'd just reached the door when he spoke again.

"Cassie."

She pivoted back to face him, her heart thumping. "What?"

"Do me a favor." His voice was soft.

She raised her brows, warily inviting specifics.

"Keep your hair down tonight. And wear a dress."

Steel entered Cassie's supple spine. "That's *two* favors, Brand," she informed him tartly.

It was an excellent exit line. Slamming the door behind her when she stalked out of his office made it even better.

Chapter Four

Hair down . . . wear a dress," Cassie muttered mutinously as she stood in front of the full-length mirror in the bedroom of her modest cottage-style home in the hills above Los Angeles. She surveyed her reflection.

Maybe even Mother would approve, she thought with an unexpected spurt of satisfaction. She tilted her head to one side and then the other. Her red-gold hair shifted over her shoulders like a silken veil, individual strands sparking to fiery life as they caught the light. She continued to study the image in the mirror. The person gazing back at her wasn't exactly a stranger, but she certainly wasn't the gawky girl Cassie tended to see in her mind's eye when she visualized herself, either.

Cassie had grown up knowing that she was never going to rival her mother in looks. Sabrina Leigh had been one of the most exquisitely lovely women of her generation. She'd been a star who'd thrived on sparkle and the spotlight. Her flawless features had photographed perfectly from all angles.

Cassie did not possess her mother's balanced beauty. While the upper half of her face was a classic oval, her jaw was slightly squared and rather stubborn. Her cheekbones were high and well-defined, with a hint of the exotic in their angularity. Yet her nose was all-American ordinary, and even turned up a tiny bit at the tip, and her ripely generous mouth didn't quite match the proportions of her other features.

Then, of course, there were her freckles. There were dozens of them and even the briefest exposure to the sun encouraged them to multiply like rabbits across her fair and fragile skin. Once when she was about ten, Cassie had tried to scrub them off with sandpaper.

As far as Cassie was concerned, her one claim to beauty was her eyes. They were wide-set and their irises were a luminous mix of gray and green. A few flecks of gold sparkled in their changeable depths. Her long, thick lashes were a soft sable brown.

Cassie pursed her lips and used the tip of one finger to smudge the kohl liner she'd applied around her eyes. The smoky shadowing added a touch of sophistication to her appearance, she decided. In fact, the extra makeup on her eyes seemed to balance the fullness of her mouth—to bring her whole face into intriguing focus.

"Not bad," she declared judiciously, then carefully picked a minute bit of lint off of the long, tightly fitted sleeves of her dress.

The matte-black silk garment was something she'd purchased on impulse several months before but had never donned since. Cut with deceptive simplicity, it discreetly revealed the graceful lines of her body before coming to a halt an inch above her kneecaps. The neckline was a demure bateau in front and a dramatic V in back.

It was the most provocative outfit Cassie had ever worn in her life. It made the most of her willowy five-foot-six-inch height, something she usually tried to play down. It also emphasized her long, showgirl-style legs—legs she normally kept covered up. And while the dress didn't hug her curves, it hinted at them in a very deliberate way.

"Not bad at all," she murmured, then tossed her head and laughed self-consciously.

The movement made the emerald drops dangling from her earlobes dance against her softly flushed cheeks. The earrings were the only jewelry she was wearing this evening. They, like the rest of the costly baubles she kept locked up in a safety deposit box, had belonged to her mother. While Cassie had never shared her mother's passion for personal adornment, she *had* inherited her love of emeralds.

She had not, until this moment, believed she'd inherited the famous Sabrina Leigh flair for wearing the green gemstones. Yet looking at herself in the mirror now, seeing herself all dressed up and ready to go, she had the feeling that maybe, just maybe—

The chime of the front doorbell diverted this uncharacteristic flow of thought. Cassie caught her breath and tried to control a tremor of anxiety. Iron butterflies began dive-bombing in the pit of her stomach. It took her a few seconds to slip her stockinged feet into a pair of strappy black evening sandals. The doorbell rang again. Squaring her shoulders and lifting her chin, Cassie went to answer its summons.

"It's show time," she whispered to herself.

"Hello," Brand greeted her pleasantly as she opened the door. He was dressed in charcoal trousers, a white shirt and an impeccably styled raw-silk jacket of black, charcoal and pearl gray. The look was a cross between California casualness and European elegance, and he wore it with an offhand, utterly masculine panache.

"Hello," Cassie responded, smoothing her dress.

"May I come in?" he requested courteously after a few moments. He smiled slightly, hinting at some inward amusement.

"Oh, yes. Please." Cassie made a quick gesture, wondering uncomfortably if she'd been staring at him. She'd seen Brand dressed for a night out many times before, of course. Still, his appearance this evening seemed particularly striking. "I'm just about ready."

"I'm a few minutes early," he replied easily as he stepped inside. Cassie caught the subtle, faintly spicy scent of his cologne as he moved by her.

There was a brief pause. Trapped somewhere between an irritating sense of self-consciousness and an inexplicable kind of excitement, Cassie lifted one hand and fluffed her hair.

"Is that a new dress?" Brand inquired.

"This?" Cassie responded, then grimaced at her own inanity. What dress did she think he meant? "Ah, no. Not really. I bought it a while ago. I just haven't had the right occasion to wear it. I mean, it's not exactly the sort of thing I'd put on for work."

"It would definitely cause a stir if you did."

Cassie wasn't certain how to react to this silken-voiced compliment. She felt more flustered than flattered by it. Finally she settled for a little laugh. It was meant to indicate she hadn't taken his remark seriously.

Then, after a fractional pause, she said, "Just let me get my purse and we can go—all right?"

"Fine."

When she returned from her bedroom about a minute later, Cassie found Brand examining his surroundings with the kind of attentiveness she'd seen him give to movie sets. He had a very knowing eye for detail. She wondered what conclusions about her character he was drawing from her decor.

She also wondered why she cared.

"You've had this place—what? About two years?" he asked.

"That's right." Shortly after beginning work at Marcus Moviemaking, she'd made up her mind that it was time for her to move out of her uncle's extremely impressive—and sometimes oppressive—Beverly Hills mansion and find a place of her own. While Jordan Addams had initially objected to her plans, he'd eventually accepted her decision. Since she'd attained her majority, and his legal guardianship of her had lapsed, he'd really had no choice in the matter.

The room Cassie and Brand were standing in was decorated in various shades of ivory and taupe and accented with shots of copper and carnelian. Most of the casually arranged furniture was comfortably contemporary, but there were a few beautiful antique pieces, too. These were part of the material legacy left by her parents. Books, video cassettes, movie memorabilia and a variety of papers were scattered about, lending a lived-in air to the place.

Brand glanced around the room once again, then smiled at Cassie. "I like it," he told her. "It suits you."

"Thank you," she replied, matching his smile with one of her own. His comment pleased her. Despite her uncle's efforts to get her to use the services of an interior designer, she'd decorated the house herself. She was happy with the result, and liked to think it reflected her true personality.

There was a short pause. Cassie fiddled briefly—and unnecessarily—with one of her emerald earrings.

"Well," Brand said, bridging the break with a characteristic combination of charm and authority, "shall we get our little show on the road?"

Cassie took a deep breath and nodded.

The first ten minutes or so of their trip passed in silence. Brand concentrated on driving, focusing his attention on the curving ribbon of road ahead as he maneuvered his expensive sports car with fluid skill. Cassie stared out the window beside her, registering very little of what she was seeing. She toyed absently with the small black-beaded evening purse sitting on her lap and tapped her foot against the floor.

She was nervous. There was no getting around the fact. She was *very* nervous. And probably even a little frightened of what she was about to attempt to do. And it didn't soothe her one bit to think about why she was going to try to—

Cassie abruptly became aware that Brand had been speaking to her. Unfortunately she'd been so preoccupied with her own thoughts that she had no idea what he'd said, nor how she was expected to reply to it.

"I'm sorry," she apologized, turning slightly to look at him. Her dress moved against her body in a whisper-light caress. Cassie was aware of the sleek glide of silk over skin. "I wasn't listening."

Brand kept his eyes on the road as he took a sharp turn, then glanced over at her. It was too dark in the car for Cassie to make out much of his expression.

"I said, you look very beautiful tonight," he told her quietly.

Cassie felt herself begin to blush. She crossed her legs, once again conscious of the sensuous stroke of the fine fabric of her dress.

"Thank you," she said after a moment or two. Her voice was a note or two higher than usual and quite a bit breathier.

Brand returned his gaze to the road ahead. "You're welcome," he replied. "But there's no need for you to sound so surprised."

Cassie blinked. "You've never said anything like that to me before," she returned with a trace of defensiveness.

"My oversight." His tone was almost identical to the one he'd used back at her house when he'd referred to the "stirring" nature of her dress. "But then, we've never been engaged before."

"We're not engaged yet," Cassie reminded him quickly.

Brand downshifted. Cassie sensed the evocative tense and release of his thigh muscles as he moved his foot from the gas pedal to the brake.

"Are you backing out?" he asked after a second. His voice was devoid of inflection. He could have been inquiring about the weather.

"No, I'm not backing out," she answered. Suddenly all the doubts she'd grappled with initially—plus all the ones she'd been ambushed by after she'd slammed out of Brand's office—coalesced into a giant knot of fear. "I just don't know if I can handle this," she confessed baldly, looking down at her hands. "Not even for *Prodigal*."

Brand shifted gears again. "You can handle anything you put your mind to, Cassie. Someday maybe you'll realize that."

"Hail, hail, the gang's all here," Brand observed with a humorless chuckle about twenty minutes later as they neared their destination. The block ahead was lined with limousines. The sidewalk in front of the restaurant where they were going was teeming with people, including a scrambling contingent from the press.

Cassie closed her eyes and wondered what she'd gotten herself into.

"Stage fright?" Brand asked her. Traffic was so snarled, he'd been forced to slow to a snail's pace.

Cassie's eyes popped open again. She glanced at the crowd gathered under the awning-covered entrance to the restaurant. "There must be four dozen reporters out there," she said. "What are we going to say to them?"

"I usually try 'no comment.' I don't want to inhibit their creativity when it comes to making up quotes."

"Brand!"

"Well, what do you tell reporters who ask you about your relationship with Chet Walker?"

"My relationship with—" Cassie's voice rose. She pulled it back down its normal register, silently damning the paparazzo who'd taken the picture of Chet's semidrunken pass at her and the tabloid editor who'd chosen to offer it as proof of a torrid romance. "Nothing," she said tautly. "I haven't said anything to the press about Chet Walker. And I'm not going to."

"You've decided pictures speak louder than words, hmm?"

For a moment, Cassie was once again tempted to tell Brand how totally wrong his assumptions about her and Chet Walker were, but she resisted the urge. Her personal life was none of his business!

"I suppose you and my uncle have discussed my relationship with Chet?" Her tone was as tart as unsweetened lemonade. She went on without waiting for a response. "You know, Brand, I never realized until this week what an expert you are about my private affairs. What have you been doing? Keeping a scrapbook?"

Brand turned into the parking lot next to the restaurant. His knuckles were white with pressure as he gripped the steering wheel.

"I'd certainly have a fair amount of material to put in it if I were, wouldn't I?" he countered, braking the car. "Given that fact, don't you think you should stop acting like a nervous virgin about tonight? After all, we both know you're no stranger to conducting your—how did you put it—your 'private affairs' in public."

"You and I are not having an affair!" Cassie gasped angrily.

His blue eyes drilled into her. "True. But we're damned well going to make everyone think we are."

The intervention of a parking lot attendant prevented Cassie from responding to this statement. She bit the inside of her lip as the young man opened the door on her side, trying to control the tiny tremors of rage running through her. The attendant handed her out with a practiced flourish and an equally practiced glance of appraisal. After shutting the door behind her, he hustled around to Brand's side of the car.

"Park it somewhere convenient, will you, Jay?" Brand requested as he got out, leaving the engine running. His voice was smooth and suavely commanding, "Miss Addams and I won't be staying long." While the words were perfectly innocent, his delivery of them was laden with innuendo.

The parking lot attendant grinned knowingly, darting another assessing look at Cassie as he deftly palmed the crisp ten-dollar bill Brand handed him. "Sure thing, Mr. Marcus," he affirmed as he slid into the driver's seat. "Your car will be ready whenever you are." He then pulled the door closed, put the sports car into gear and headed it smoothly toward the nearest open parking slot.

Cassie crossed to Brand, the heels of her sandals clicking out an indignant rhythm on the asphalt. "Was that really necessary?" she hissed.

A soft night breeze stirred her hair. Brand reached forward and brushed a stray strand off her flushed cheek. Cassie jerked away from his touch, glaring at him.

He brought his hand back down to his side. "Yes, it was necessary."

"Why?"

"Because," he responded in a low, precise voice, "Jay doesn't just earn tips. He also supplies them to several tabloids." His eyes narrowed dangerously, then focused on her mouth. "Why don't we give him a really juicy tidbit to report?"

Cassie's heart lurched at his tone. She opened her mouth to speak.

Brand reached for her. "Close your eyes, sweetheart," he instructed softly. "I'm going to kiss you."

It was characteristic of Brand that he swiftly followed words with action. It was also characteristic of him that he took ruthlessly erotic advantage of the fact that Cassie's lips were parted on the beginning of a protest as his closed over them.

Brand controlled the kiss from start to finish, mastering Cassie's instinctive resistance, then encouraging the equally instinctive response that blossomed in its wake. He feathered the fingers of one hand along the line of her jaw, then wove them deep into the heavy tumble of her hair. Tilting her head back, he increased his access to her mouth and deepened the seal of his sensual possession.

Cassie felt Brand's other hand sweep up her spine. His touch was swift and sure. She shuddered, making a tiny sound deep in her throat as he stroked from silk to bare skin.

She was falling. Tumbling...tumbling...like Alice through the Looking Glass. She was careering headlong into an unexplored world where everything familiar seemed strange and everything unfamiliar seemed infinitely seductive.

Cassie was aware of the brief but heady intrusion of Brand's tongue as he sought and savored the sweet inner flesh of her mouth. She made another whimpering sound.

And then, suddenly, the kiss was over.

Brand lifted his head, freeing her lips. His breathing was harsh and uneven, and his eyes had darkened to a stormy midnight. There was a flush of color along the arrogant line of his cheekbones.

The ground seemed to tilt beneath Cassie's feet. She would have collapsed, her knees giving way like overcooked pasta, if Brand hadn't steadied her. She wanted to cling to him.

She'd been kissed before, of course. And quite thoroughly on several occasions. But she'd never experienced anything like the past few moments with Brand. Never. Ever.

"B-Brand?" She spoke his name in a shaky whisper.

Cassie watched Brand take several slow breaths. She could see him rebuilding his self-control piece by piece. When he finished the job, his manner was as smooth and as impenetrable as a marble wall. He was back in charge of himself, and the situation.

"Brand?" she repeated, a bit more strongly. Pride forced her to shake off his supportive hand and pull the tatters of her own poise into some kind of order.

Brand's lips parted. There was a flash of white teeth. But the expression on his face could not be called a smile. Nor was there anything remotely pleasant about the look in his eyes.

"Earlier today, you told me you weren't a very good actress," he said huskily. "You're a lot better than you think, Cassie."

Chapter Five

They stayed at the birthday party for less than two hours. Brand glided through the glittering festivities with easy, enviable aplomb. Cassie operated on automatic pilot, experiencing a curious kind of detachment as she said and did all the necessary social things.

This detachment didn't mean she wasn't feeling anything. Quite the contrary. Throughout the evening, Cassie had the strange sense that, deep down, she was feeling *too* much. It was as though a protective mechanism she hadn't known she possessed had disconnected her emotions from her awareness of them in order to save her from some sort of psychological overload.

They returned to her house shortly after midnight. The ride home from the party was even more silent than the one to it had been. And there was a different quality to the silence. It was intimate...and unsettling. While she and Brand scarcely exchanged a word during the entire drive, Cassie had the disturbing impression that they were communicating at a very basic, nonverbal level.

Brand walked her to her front door. The cool night breeze fingered her silk dress and ruffled his dark hair. The dim illumination from the Japanese-style lantern by the door reduced Brand's striking features to a compelling study in highlighted planes and shadowed hollows.

Brand was the first one to speak.

"I'll drive you to the studio in the morning," he said without preamble. It was not an offer.

"I'm quite capable of getting myself to work, thank you," she responded immediately. Her refusal was more than an instinctive bridling against his autocratic assertion.

"I've already conceded that I think you're capable of just about anything, Cassie," he returned without missing a beat. "I still expect you to be ready when I come by for you at seven forty-five."

Cassie stiffened. "Is this how you treat your women?" she demanded, lifting her chin challengingly. "Always ordering them around?"

Brand's eyes widened slightly and one corner of his mouth twitched. Cassie sensed that her blunt—and probably ill-advised—question both startled and amused him.

"Actually, no," he drawled. "Most of 'my women,' as you call them, do what I want them to without being told."

Cassie's face flamed. "Well, I'm very sorry to disappoint you," she flashed back in a tone that indicated exactly the opposite.

The twitch of Brand's mobile mouth became a mocking smile. "No, you're not," he said. "But it doesn't matter. We both know you're not one of my women. In any case, you don't disappoint me."

He paused, his eyes roving over her upturned face as though taking an inventory of her flushed features. Cassie felt her color deepen in response to his scrutiny.

"You get under my skin sometimes," he continued thoughtfully. "And you've surprised the hell out of me on more than a few occasions. But you don't disappoint me."

His voice softened on the last sentence, and his gaze settled slowly, deliberately, on her mouth.

For one heart-pounding instant, Cassie was afraid he was going to kiss her again. What was worse, she was afraid she *wanted* him to kiss her again—that she'd *been* wanting him to ever since that erotically expert kiss in the parking lot.

"Brand—" she began breathlessly. She sounded as though she was pleading. But pleading for what?

She must have shaken her head or taken a step back without realizing it, because something about him changed almost before his name left her lips. Whether it was his expression or his stance or something else that altered, Cassie wasn't sure. But whatever it was that had made her believe she was in danger of being kissed by him—and "danger" definitely seemed the right word—it vanished.

"Is seven forty-five all right with you?" he asked quietly.

Cassie gave in, but not completely. "Eight would be better," she countered.

A glint of admiration appeared in Brand's eyes. The tension between them seemed to ease. "Eight, it is," he agreed. Then after brushing her still-pinkened cheek with one careless finger, he turned to leave.

"Brand?" Cassie thought her voice was back to normal, or something very close to it.

"Mmm?" He pivoted back to face her, his brows arched in inquiry.

"It...it worked tonight, didn't it?" she asked tentatively. It suddenly seemed very important to remind herself—to remind both of them—of what was really going on.

An odd look flitted across Brand's face. "Well, we should get some early reviews of our performances in tomorrow's gossip columns," he replied. "But as far as I could tell, we made a good start. And going in to work together in the morning will help the cause."

"You know what people will think."

"Exactly what we want them to think. And it won't be that we've decided to conserve energy by carpooling."

"No," she concurred wryly. "It won't."

"Anything else?"

Cassie hesitated, uncomfortably aware of a desire to prolong this encounter. "No," she said after a moment. "That's all."

"Of course, the accomodations leave a lot to be desired, too," Brand declared shortly after eight-thirty the next morning. He flicked on the car's right turn signal. "We're going to be stuck dividing the L.A. crew between two motels. Both of them are at least an hour's drive from most of our main locations. One has a pool, thank God. But the owner of that place wants cash up front because she doesn't trust show—Cassie?"

Brand took his eyes off the road for a moment. Although he was wearing mirrored sunglasses, there was no missing the sharpness of the glance he gave her.

Cassie covered her mouth with her right hand and tried, not very successfully, to smother a yawn. "Mm-mmphf?" she responded through her fingers.

"Am I boring you?"

"Ah-h-h-h—" Cassie forced herself to swallow the tail end of the yawn. "No, not at all," she assured him with complete honesty. The behind-the-scenes nitty-gritty of moviemaking had always fascinated her far more than the glamorous razzle-dazzle most people associated with the film industry.

"Then what is it?"

Cassie fought down another yawn. Her red-gold hair was back in its usual workday braid. As she took her hand away from her mouth, she trailed her fingers along the length of the plait, then twisted the end of it.

"I didn't get much sleep last night," she admitted.

"Not much" actually meant almost none. Normally Cassie drifted peacefully off to sleep as soon as her head hit the pillow. But she'd tossed and turned for hours after getting into bed the previous night. Once she'd finally fallen asleep, she'd been troubled by dreams.

Dreams about Brand.

"I see" was all he said.

They rode on without speaking for several minutes. Cassie brushed several small pieces of lint off her corduroy slacks and fiddled with one of the buttons on the loose-fitting plaid shirt she'd belted over a dark brown cotton top. She sighed heavily.

For a brief period, as they'd been discussing some of the preproduction work for *Prodigal*, things had seemed to be back to normal between her and Brand. Well, almost back to normal, she amended. There was nothing "normal" about her acute awareness of the man sitting to her left.

Cassie glanced sideways. Brand was dressed in running shoes, faded jeans and a navy turtleneck. She'd seen him wearing the same clothes dozens of times before. Yet this morning, they seemed different.

For the first time, she was conscious of how the wash-softened denim of Brand's jeans hugged his muscled thighs and emphasized his masculinity. For the first time, she found herself unable to ignore the way the snug-fitting pullover underscored the powerful symmetry of his upper body.

Cassie had always been aware that Brandon Marcus was an attractive man. She wasn't blind. She wasn't insensitive. And she certainly wasn't as oblivious to the obvious as he'd suggested the day before! But she'd never experienced the tug of attraction she was experiencing now.

In some inexplicable way, she felt as though she was seeing Brand from a totally new perspective. He suddenly seemed so much more vivid to her. So much more male. So much more . . . *more*.

She didn't understand it! She'd known Brand for two years. She'd worked by his side for six months. Yet the man she was looking at now was almost a stranger to her. He was not the same man she'd agreed to pretend to become engaged to. He was different. He'd changed.

Or perhaps *she* was the one who'd changed?

This last thought popped into Cassie's head unbidden and she shoved it out as though it were radioactive. She was being ridiculous. She'd allowed herself to be placed in an incredibly awkward position and now she was overreacting. That was all!

Or was it?

Yes, Brand had kissed her. And, yes, she'd responded to him. But that didn't mean that she was—

"Cassie?"

The sound of her name jerked Cassie back into the present. She came to the swift and uncomfortable realization that she'd been staring at Brand's profile for several minutes.

"What?" she snapped, trying to hide her embarrassment.

Brand didn't take his eyes off the road. "Do you think you would have slept better if I'd said I was sorry I kissed you in the parking lot?" he inquired mildly.

Cassie was so surprised by this question that she blurted out the first thing that came into her head. "You've never apologized to me for anything you've done!"

There was a short silence. Cassie spent it wishing she could recall the words she'd spoken so impetuously.

"There's a first time for everything," Brand remarked after a few moments, appearing to accept her tactless—although essentially accurate—comment with an unusual degree of forbearance. "Maybe the prospect of becoming engaged has inspired me to turn over a new leaf. Like my complimenting you on the way you looked last night. You said I'd never done that before, either."

Cassie swallowed, trying not to remember how she'd felt when Brand had told her she was beautiful.

"Why should you want to apologize for kissing me?" she questioned, wishing he would take off his sunglasses. Brand was not an easy man to read under the best of circumstances, but she'd found that his eyes usually provided some clue as to what was going on inside his head. "You said we were going to convince everyone we're having an affair. I thought the kiss was—was—" She searched for the appropriate phrase, and latched on to something he'd said the day before. "I thought the kiss was part of the scenario."

"Cassie, I—" Brand paused, turning the car onto the wide, tree-lined boulevard that led to the main gate of the Phoenix Studio.

Had it been anyone else but Brand, Cassie would have described the pause as a hesitation. But it *was* Brand. In all the time she'd known him, she'd never seen him hesitate about anything.

The pause lengthened to the point of awkwardness and beyond.

"Brand?" she finally asked.

"Things got a little out of control last night," he declared, speaking as though there'd been no break in the conversation. "I was angry. It won't happen again."

Something about the tone of this assertion stung Cassie. "What won't happen again? You getting angry? Or you kissing me?"

Brand downshifted and gave her another swift glance. Again she wished she could see the eyes behind the impenetrable, vaguely intimidating sunglasses.

"As long as you're around," he replied dryly, "I'm bound to get angry now and then. And I'm afraid that this act we're putting on is going to require some kissing and touching if it's going to be persuasive. But the loss of control won't happen again. You have my word on that."

Any desire Cassie might have had to pursue this subject—and she wasn't at all sure she wanted to explore it any further—was curbed by their arrival at the main studio gate.

"Mornin', Mr. Marcus. Mornin', Cassie." These greetings came from the grizzled old-timer who had been on morning duty at the Phoenix front entrance for nearly three decades.

"Good morning," Brand responded.

"Hi, Joe," Cassie chimed in.

"That's sure a nice picture of the two of you this morning," the guard remarked cheerfully. "Real nice."

"Picture?" Cassie echoed. Her stomach fluttered nervously. "What picture?"

Joe glanced back and forth between Cassie and Brand, obviously surprised. "The one in the paper. You mean you haven't seen it yet? Well, hey. Take my copy." Turning away from them for a moment, he extracted a somewhat dog-eared newspaper from beneath a disorganized stack of things on the small counter inside his guard's booth. "Sorry it's kind of wrinkled," he apologized as he handed the paper to Brand.

Whether by accident or design, the paper was folded so the picture of Cassie and Brand was facing outward. Brand glanced at it quickly, his mouth twisting a little.

"Thank you, Joe," he said as he turned the paper over to Cassie.

"My pleasure, Mr. Marcus. Like I said. It's a nice picture of the two of you. Not like some that get printed."

Cassie didn't say anything. She was too busy staring at the paper. In fact, she was only dimly aware of Brand putting the car back into gear and driving onto the studio lot after receiving Joe's usual admonition to have a good day.

The photograph held her eyes the way a magnet holds iron. It showed her and Brand going into the previous night's party. His arm was draped possessively around her waist and he was smiling down at her. She was looking up at him, her expression almost dazed.

As she studied the black-and-white photo, Cassie found herself remembering the way her mouth had tingled from the demanding pressure of his. She recalled how warm and strong his lean fingers had felt as they'd pressed against the fine material of her dress.

You're a better actress than you think, Brand had told her.

Perhaps this was true. But the way she was staring at him in the picture—and the way she'd been feeling at the instant it had been taken—had nothing to do with acting.

It had nothing to do with reality, either.

"'Nice,'" she muttered unhappily, staring down at the paper.

"I take it that's not the adjective you'd use?" Brand inquired blandly.

Cassie's head came up with a jerk, her thick braid bouncing against her breast. "Do *you* think this is a 'nice' picture?"

Brand maneuvered his car skillfully into his reserved parking space. "I've seen better of both of us," he answered. "And I've seen worse. But in terms of the impression we're trying to create, it's very effective."

"You mean it speaks for itself," she returned with an edge.

Brand's fingers tightened on the steering wheel for just an instant, then relaxed. "Exactly," he agreed as he shut off the car's engine. "It speaks for itself. Just like the picture of you and Chet Walker."

And just like that picture, she thought furiously, everything it's supposed to be saying is a lie!

Cassie unfastened her seat belt with fingers that weren't quite steady, then leaned forward to grab her canvas tote bag. Straightening, she flipped her braid over her shoulder with a toss of her head and reached for the door handle.

"Cassie."

She froze, then glanced over at Brand. He still hadn't taken off his sunglasses. "What now?"

"You might try a slightly more pleasant expression," he advised. "We're trying to establish ourselves as a couple, remember? It's a little early to be seen having our first fight."

Cassie summoned up a smile that was as incandescent as it was insincere. "If memory serves, Brand," she said sweetly, "we had our first fight six months ago. It was during my second week as your personal assistant."

"If memory serves, sweetheart," he replied, "our first fight was during your second *hour* as my personal assistant."

Chapter Six

Three very long weeks later, Cassie sat at her desk wondering what would happen if she hung up on her uncle.

"Cassie—"

"Uncle Jordan, please!"

"I care about you, honey."

Cassie massaged her right temple. Her uncle had shifted into his loving but long-suffering mode several minutes before. There was a nicely calculated hint of weariness in his voice. Its purpose, she knew, was to reveal to her how burdened with avuncular concern he was. He sounded slightly wounded, too. This, no doubt, was a bid to make her feel guilty about not confiding in him.

She felt guilty, all right. But her refusal to tell her uncle what was really going on in her life was only a small part of that emotion.

"I know you care about me," she said, wedging the phone between her left ear and shoulder. "And I care about you. But I'm not a little girl anymore. My personal life is—is—"

"Your personal life is all over the papers!" her uncle informed her in an outraged tone.

"Do you think I like it?" she flung back. It was the first unguarded response she'd made since the start of their conversation.

"Cassie...Cassie...Cassie." She could visualize her uncle shaking his head and stroking his palm against his rapidly thinning hair. She heard him sigh. When he spoke again, his voice was shorn of all efforts to manipulate.

"Look, honey, I know I've been a little heavy-handed with you in the past," he acknowledged, then chuckled ruefully. "Okay. Okay. Maybe a *lot* heavy-handed. But I've been trying to do better. I didn't say a word when that picture of you and Brand turned up in the tabloids a couple of weeks back. Same thing when I started seeing your names linked in the columns. And I thought I was pretty restrained a few nights ago when I ran into the two of you at that fund-raiser for the rain forests."

"Yes, you were," Cassie agreed uncomfortably. She decided not to remind him that he'd phoned her at six the morning after the fund-raiser in an obvious effort to determine a) whether she'd spent the night in her own bed, and b) if she had, whether she had done so alone.

"So all right," he went on. "I've been trying. But, dammit, Cassie, I can't keep quiet after the item in this morning's Telling All column. I'm supposed to fly to New York in less than two hours. There's no way I can leave L.A. without finding out what's going on. So to hell with my trying to do better. The column says wedding bells. Has Brand Marcus proposed to you?"

Cassie swallowed. She'd known she was going to have to face this kind of cross-examination from her uncle sooner or later. Frankly she was astonished he'd waited so long to start asking questions. Her colleagues at work had been grilling her—with various degrees of finesse—for days.

"Not exactly," she said very carefully.

"Not exactly?"

"We've talked about getting engaged." Cassie tried to comfort herself with the thought that this was not a lie. Yes, it created a totally misleading impression, but it was *not* a lie. Brand and she *had* spoken about getting engaged.

"You've 'talked' about it."

Something in her uncle's tone sent a shiver of apprehension running through Cassie.

"You know," he continued ominously, "maybe Brand and *I* should talk about—"

"No!" The word erupted out of her.

There was a stunned silence on the other end of the line. Cassie suddenly realized that she'd surged to her feet when she'd yelled into the telephone. Trembling, she sank back into her chair.

"Cassie—"

"No, Uncle Jordan!" she cut in swiftly, shaking her head vehemently. "I don't want you talking to Brand about this. Do you hear me? I don't want you talking to him!"

Her uncle harrumphed. "Cassandra Leigh, I think I have a right to ask the man what his intentions are," he declared stiffly.

The resentment that had been smoldering within Cassie for three weeks caught flame. "You already know what his intentions are!" she retorted.

There was another silence on the other end of the line.

"What, exactly, is that supposed to mean?" her uncle finally asked.

Cassie rubbed her eyes, debating what she could—and should—say in reply. After several seconds, she decided she had to finish what she'd started.

"Not too long after Brand promoted me," she said steadily, "you had a talk with him about a rumor that he and I were sleeping together. He denied the rumor. He also said any intentions he had toward me were honorable ones."

"You know about that?" Jordan Addams sounded astonished and more than a little embarrassed.

"Yes."

"Brand told you?"

"Yes."

"Well, I'll be..."

"Probably."

Her uncle muttered something unintelligible, then said, "I did it for your own good, honey." His words were as much an apology as an excuse.

Cassie sighed. "I know."

"I don't want you to get hurt. I'd do anything to prevent that. *Anything*."

"I know that, too."

"This situation with you and Brand—"

"I know what I'm doing, Uncle Jordan. Please, believe me. I know what I'm doing."

It was, Cassie reflected, a futile request at best. How could she expect anyone to believe that she knew what she was doing when she, herself, no longer found it possible to do so?

Cassie said goodbye to her uncle several minutes later. She dropped the phone receiver back into its cradle. What next? she wondered with a hint of black humor.

She was fairly certain she'd deterred her former guardian from taking any immediate action where she and Brand were concerned. Unfortunately she was even more certain that she'd failed to defuse his explosively overprotective instincts. Some kind of blowup was inevitable and there was no telling what would trigger it. A comment. A photograph. An item in a gossip column...

Cassie's eyes strayed to the newspaper sitting on the left-hand corner of her desk. After a moment's hesitation, she reached for it.

There was no need for her to leaf through the publication. She'd left it folded open to the relevant page. And there was no need for her to scan through any copy. She'd circled the salient paragraph of that day's Telling All column with a ballpoint pen.

"Also seen billing and cooing at last night's big bash," ran the gushing prose, "were Oscar-winning director Brandon Marcus and his personal assistant, Cassandra Addams. Cassie's parents were screen queen Sabrina Leigh and movie mogul Christopher Addams. She's the niece of superagent Jordan Addams and former flame of bad-boy actor Chet Walker."

Cassie grimaced her distaste at the last part of the sentence, then went on skimming the words she had long since learned by heart.

"The couple came late, left early and had eyes only for each other all evening," the piece continued breathlessly. "Brand's next film—*Prodigal*—remains uncast. But an insider at Marcus Moviemaking whispers that, after personally auditioning a long, long list of lovelies, the filmmaker has finally found his real-life leading lady. We're listening for wedding bells!"

Cassie shook her head. She couldn't blame her uncle for being upset by the item. Lord knew, she'd felt more than a little shocked when *she'd* read it the first time. So, she'd gathered, had quite a few of her colleagues at Marcus Moviemaking.

There was no doubting the effectiveness of the performance she and Brand had been putting on during the past three weeks. They had deliberately set out to establish themselves as one of Hollywood's hottest couples, and they had done so.

The problem was, the flurry of publicity about their supposed relationship apparently hadn't impressed the one person it was meant to. So far there'd been no indication that Graham Wyatt was aware his wife's ex-lover was involved in a new romance.

Cassie closed her eyes for a moment.

We've got seven weeks before principal photography starts on Prodigal, Brand had told her. *That should give us more than enough time to convince Graham Wyatt and everybody else that we're an item.*

And if it's not? she'd asked.

If we get to within three weeks of the start date and I don't have Graham's name on a contract, we'll look at the alternatives.

Cassie opened her eyes. They were now seven days away from the deadline Brand had set. Just one short week to go.

Brand *had* heard from Sheila Parker. That much Cassie knew for certain. She'd seen a phone message slip with Sheila's name on it and she was sure the call had been returned. But she had no idea of what Mrs. Graham Wyatt had said to her former lover, nor he to her. Brand hadn't volunteered any information about the conversation and she certainly hadn't pressed the issue with him.

Cassie sighed heavily and shifted in her chair. After a few restless seconds, she picked up a pen from the clutter on her desk. She began doodling around the edges of the Telling All column.

What if it's all been for nothing? she asked herself starkly. What if the past three weeks don't matter?

With an inarticulate sound of distress and frustration, Cassie hurled her pen across the room. At the same instant, the door to her tiny office swung open and Brand looked in. The ballpoint missed his head by a scant two inches.

Brand didn't flinch. "Maybe I should have worn a target," he suggested with sardonic calm as he stepped into her small work space.

Cassie's cheeks blazed with embarrassment. "Maybe you should have knocked!"

He bent to pick up the pen. "Actually, I did," he informed her as he straightened. "Apparently you didn't hear me."

Cassie's shoulders sagged a little. She didn't dispute Brand's assertion. It was all too plausible.

Brand came toward her, moving with the lithe, powerful stride that was so much a part of him. His dynamic male presence seemed to fill the small confines of her work space. He was wearing jeans and a fraying wash-faded sweatshirt with chopped-off sleeves. His sunglasses had been carelessly shoved on top of his head, messing up dark hair that was several weeks overdue for a trim.

"What's wrong, Cassie?" he questioned abruptly, dropping the pen he'd picked up into the clutter on top of her desk. While his attire was casual, the expression on his face was not.

"Nothing's wrong," she replied immediately, trying to keep any hint of defensiveness out of her voice. She had to lift her chin to look him in the eye. The arrogant assurance of his posture and the leanly athletic lines of his body made him seem even taller than his actual six-foot height.

"You look tired."

Cassie suppressed a sigh. She was beyond tired. She was absolutely exhausted. In truth, she hadn't had a peaceful night's sleep in weeks. And her emotions had been playing havoc with her appetite, as well.

But she couldn't tell Brand any of that. She felt too vulnerable to him as it was. She wasn't about to make even the slightest admission of weakness.

"It's all the partying we've been doing," she replied, leaning forward a little to point to the newspaper article she'd practically obliterated with her scribbling. "We made today's Telling All column."

"I know." Brand eyed her wordlessly for several seconds, then asked, "Is the publicity getting to you, Cassie?"

"No," she denied automatically, shaking her head. Her heavy braid swung back and forth. "Anyway, publicity is what we want, isn't it?" She glanced down at the newspaper and wrinkled her nose. "I will concede I could have done without the reference to Chet Walker."

"So could I." Brand followed his arms across his chest.

His tone puzzled Cassie. She studied him for a moment, then decided it was wiser not to ask for an explanation. "You wouldn't happen to know the identity of the Marcus

Moviemaking insider who's been whispering about us, would you?" she inquired.

Brand shrugged. "I'd say the list of suspects is fairly long," he answered noncommittally, then frowned. "Is that bothering you? All the gossip around the office?"

"It's hard," Cassie admitted slowly. "Everybody's curious. I understand that."

"But you're getting tired of the questions and comments."

She spread her hands, palms up. "I'm not as good at handling them as you are."

"Meaning I'm the more accomplished liar."

"I didn't say that."

"You don't have to," he replied with a faint edge. "Making believe—making things up—is part of my profession."

Cassie remained silent for several seconds. There had been a number of times during the past three weeks when she'd been as appalled as she was astonished by the glib way Brand fielded inquiries about their relationship. Once or twice she'd found herself wondering if he'd rehearsed the words beforehand.

She'd found herself wondering about the preparation behind other aspects of his public behavior, as well. The way he reached for her whenever they were within touching distance. The way his eyes sought hers when they were not. How much did he plan those things? And what about the way he spoke her name? Teasingly, tenderly, as though the sound of it was infinitely precious to him. Did he practice that?

She knew it was all absolutely calculated. All utterly controlled. It was an act from start to finish.

And yet, he was so convincing. Sometimes she felt herself beginning to believe—

"Cassie?"

She started, then shook her head to clear it. "Did you have some reason for coming in here, Brand?" she asked abruptly. She gave him a quick, sharp glance, then dropped her gaze to her desk. She started to tidy up the clutter that covered it. "I've really got a lot of work to do."

"Graham Wyatt called."

Cassie's busy hands stilled. Slowly she raised her eyes to his. "Why—why didn't you say when you came in?"

"I was too busy ducking your pen."

Cassie grimaced. She let a second or two pass, expecting Brand to go on speaking. He didn't. "Well?" she prompted edgily. "What did he want?"

"He's invited us to visit him and Sheila in Palm Springs."

"To talk about doing *Prodigal*?"

Brand nodded. It was impossible to tell what was going on inside his head.

Cassie's gaze moved from Brand's face, to the newspaper on her desk and back again. Her heart was pounding and her palms were damp. "When?"

"This weekend."

"The *whole* weekend?" Cassie's anxiety level skyrocketed.

"Do you have something better to do?"

The question grated on her. For one none-too-rational moment, Cassie wondered how Brand would react if she told him she did. Judging from the tone of his question, she suspected he'd have no compunction about ordering her to cancel whatever plans she'd made.

"Do you?" he repeated.

Goaded by the sudden memory of his comment about the woman who did what he wanted without being told, she answered, "I was going to wash my hair."

"You can wash your hair in Palm Springs," he returned flatly, then frowned. "Do you have anything decent to wear? Graham mentioned something about a dinner party on Saturday night."

It took Cassie a second to accept that she'd actually heard his inquiry correctly. "Of course I have something decent to wear!" she snapped.

"I hope you're not thinking about that black silk dress you wore three weeks ago."

The statement caught her completely offguard. "Why? What's wrong with it?"

"The back is an open invitation to assault."

"You said that dress was beautiful!"

"I said *you* were beautiful" came the swift, almost savage correction. "And it was just the two of us when I said it."

Cassie opened her mouth to respond, then shut it when she realized she'd temporarily lost the ability to speak.

"I don't want you wearing that dress in Palm Springs," Brand went on. "I don't want you wearing it again, period."

Indignation restored Cassie's voice. "Well, what if I want to wear it again? I got a lot of compliments on that dress, Brand."

"And more than a few come-ons."

She gaped at him, taken aback by both what he'd said and the way he'd said it. "What are you talking about? I didn't notice—"

"Dammit, Cassie, there are a lot of things you don't notice!"

There was a disastrous silence. Cassie stared up at Brand, shaken to the core by the force of his outburst. He stared back at her, eyes blazing, lips pressed together as though he was fighting to hold a torrent of words in check.

Cassie could never accurately calculate how long the silence lasted. It was not the kind of break in a conversation that could be described in terms of seconds or minutes.

Finally Brand sucked in a deep breath and glanced away from her. Cassie saw him clench and unclench his hands several times. He expelled the breath he'd taken.

"I'm sorry," he said finally, his gaze still averted. His voice was tight.

"It's... it's all right," Cassie replied. She didn't know what else to say. She folded her hands beneath her desk. They were shaking.

Brand looked at her again. "No," he contradicted grimly, "it's not. I have no right to tell you what you can—or can't—wear. I apologize."

There was a short pause.

"Apology accepted," Cassie said after a few moments. "And I won't take the black dress to Palm Springs."

Brand winced as though he'd just taken a blow. "If you want to take it—"

"It would be tacky to wear it again so soon," she improvised quickly, wanting to get off the subject of the black silk dress. "I mean, I'm sure Sheila and Graham saw the picture of me in it. I wouldn't want them to think it's the only thing I own." She manufactured a little laugh, then chattered on as rapidly as she could. "So... a dinner party Saturday night?"

Cassie tried to visualize the contents of her closet. It was hard for her to think clearly, so it took her a while to sort through the jumbled images. "I have the outfit I wore to Uncle Jordan's New Year's Eve party," she murmured after nearly thirty seconds.

"The green-and-gold dress with the ruffles?"

Cassie blinked, startled by the accuracy of his description. "You remember what I had on?"

Brand nodded.

"You didn't like it?" Although she'd certainly never admit it to Brand at this juncture, Cassie didn't particularly like the dress in question, either. She'd been talked into buying it by one of her uncle's relentlessly trendy lady friends and a persuasively chic saleswoman.

Brand seemed to consider his response very carefully. "I've never thought of you as being the fuss and flourishes type, Cassie," he finally replied.

"I see." Cassie had a sudden urge to ask him exactly what type he *had* thought of her as being, but she squelched it.

"Maybe you should take a break and go shopping," Brand suggested suddenly. He rubbed the back of his neck with one hand. "You could use some time away from the office. A few hours on Rodeo Drive should be all you need."

A few hours on Rodeo Drive? Cassie recoiled at the thought. Rodeo Drive, probably the choicest address in Beverly Hills's prestigious shopping district, was an area she did her best to avoid. It was partly a matter of being indifferent to the glamour Rodeo Drive had to offer. It was partly a matter of being intimidated by it, as well.

"I hate shopping," she declared flatly.

"Well, would you like me to go with you?" Brand inquired after a moment, making the offer as though it were the most natural thing in the world.

"Would I like you to— No! Of course not!" Cassie shook her head, making her braid swing wildly. A dozen different emotions combined to paint her cheeks with hot, embarrassed color. Her entire body grew warm at the thought of what it would be like to have Brand waiting and watching as she paraded in and out of dressing rooms, modeling various outfits.

What in the name of heaven could have possessed him to make such a suggestion? she wondered. Less than five minutes before, he'd been storming at her like a...a...oh, like a she didn't know what! His comments about her little black dress and the response he claimed it had provoked had been as inexplicable as they'd been intemperate. Yet now he was radiating sunshine and goodwill and offering to take her shopping!

Cassie had seen a lot of men looking at clothes with their wives and girlfriends. Most of them had seemed uncomfortable or bored or both. But a few had plainly considered shopping a kind of courtship ritual—a time for covert touches and flirtatious banter.

She knew, with sudden and absolute certainty, that Brandon Marcus was a member of the latter group. He was a man who appreciated a healthy show of feminine vanity. He was also a man who gave the impression that he would take almost as much pleasure in watching a woman put on a piece of clothing as he would in taking it off her.

Cassie swallowed, praying that her face wasn't betraying the direction of her thoughts.

"It was just an idea." Although his acceptance of her rejection was casual, the expression in his eyes was anything but. He was studying her with unnerving intensity. The stroke of his gaze over her face was as tangible as a physical touch.

"Well, I appreciate the offer," Cassie returned, trying to match his offhand tone. "But I'd really rather do it myself. Thank you."

"All right. Fine." Brand made a gesture of acquiescence. "Just make sure to give me the receipts so I can reimburse you."

"I will not." Her response was instant, indignant and unequivocal.

"Cassie—"

"No!" she refused. "Look, I'll go shopping if that's what you want, Brand. But I can pay for my clothes as well as pick them out."

There was a long pause. Finally Brand tilted his head to one side. "Most women I know wouldn't turn down the offer of a free dress," he observed in a neutral voice.

"Well, I'm not 'most' women."

Brand thrust his hands into his jeans pockets and rocked back on his heels. "So I've noticed."

"And what's *that* supposed to mean?"

"I'm not sure," he answered with a hint of mockery. It was impossible to tell exactly what—or whom—he was mocking.

Another silence, this one knotted and awkward, formed between them.

What is going on? Cassie asked herself. Why was it that so many of the conversations she and Brand had had during the past three weeks had ended up bristling with unexplained tensions and double meanings? Why did the most innocuous of subjects—the most mundane of comments—keep blowing up as though they'd been booby-trapped with some type of emotional explosive? And why was it that the more aware of Brand she became, the more of an enigma he seemed?

It wasn't just the stress and strain of the lie they were living, she decided. That was a big part of the problem, of course; but there was something else influencing the situation, as well. Something that ran much deeper and was much more dangerous.

Cassie came to her feet in an abrupt movement.

"You're not sure?" she echoed, tossing her head. "Well, Brand, do alert me when you finally figure it out."

He gave her an ironic nod. "You'll be the second to know."

Chapter Seven

Brand and Cassie went to a movie that evening. Afterward they went out for pizza.

The "movie" was a private screening of a new comedy film. The "pizza" was the specialty of the house at one of Los Angeles's most popular restaurants.

"I can't believe the studio's actually going to release that picture," Cassie commented with a shake of her head after the waiter had served their meal. Although the menu offered pizzas garnished with such exotic and expensive items as beluga caviar, smoked goat cheese and imported foie gras, she and Brand had opted for the more traditional toppings of pepperoni and mushrooms.

Brand flashed her a smile and took a swallow of the robust red wine they'd ordered. "What? You don't think it's going to get two thumbs up?" he questioned mockingly, referring to the rating method employed by two of television's most famous movie reviewers.

"I think the critics are going to be too busy holding their noses to bother doing much with their thumbs," Cassie replied trenchantly. "You know, if I'd made a movie like that—"

"Which you wouldn't."

She laughed a little. "Thank you for the vote of confidence. But if I had, I'd steal the negative, burn it and bury the ashes."

Brand lifted his brows. "That's not what you told the producer."

"True," Cassie acknowledged, brushing a wavy lock of hair back behind her shoulder with the sweep of one hand. "I told him I'd never seen anything like his film before. Which, thank heaven, I haven't."

Cassie had not expected to enjoy this night out. Neither, she suspected, had Brand. Although he'd slipped into his public role as her attentive and affectionate escort with infuriating ease when they'd arrived at the screening, he'd seem preoccupied. And while she'd concentrated on playing her part in their romantic charade, she'd felt more fraudulent than ever.

Strangely enough, the unadulterated awfulness of the screening had broken the tension between them and rescued the night from disaster. About ten minutes after the garish opening titles, Brand had suddenly leaned close to her and whispered a devastating one-line critique of the witless scene they were watching. The remark had tickled her sense of humor. The fan of his warm breath against her cheek had made her tingle.

Acting purely on instinct, Cassie had turned her head and responded with a murmured quip of her own. She'd heard Brand chuckle deep in his chest, and caught a glimpse of a boldly appreciative smile.

A few minutes later, he'd leaned close again and whispered another scathingly witty comment. There had been no danger of him disturbing the other members of the audience. Many of them were chattering back and forth. Some were groaning in obvious distress. A few were staring silently at the screen with expressions of appalled fascination. Cassie eventually whispered to Brand that she suspected these fortunate few had been rendered temporarily deaf by the picture's painfully overamplified soundtrack.

She'd been weak with hilarity by the time the lights in the screening room had gone up. The film's producer had seen this and chosen to interpret it as a good sign. Cassie hadn't had the heart to tell him why she'd been laughing so much.

"Mitch Elliott took what you said to him as a compliment, you realize," Brand commented, cutting her a wedge of pizza.

"Well, you know how producers are," Cassie answered. She took a greedy bite of the slice he'd given her, savoring the zestily spiced tomato sauce and the yeasty richness of the freshly baked crust.

"Mmm. Always trying to make chicken salad out of chicken you-know-what."

Cassie chewed and swallowed, then took a quick sip of wine. "What about what you said to Mitch?" she challenged teasingly.

"I believe I said I didn't know what to say."

"He took that as a compliment, too. Imagine. A comedy that leaves Oscar-winning screenwriter-director Brandon Marcus speechless!" she laughed. "You really couldn't find the words to describe it, hmm?"

He turned toward her. They were seated side by side at one of the six leather-covered banquettes that were regarded as the restaurant's prime tables. Brand's leanly muscled leg brushed Cassie's slender one for an instant. He adjusted his position again and their knees bumped.

"Oh, I could find the words," he said acerbically. "I just didn't think they were appropriate for mixed company."

"How very considerate of you," Cassie joked lightly, trying to ignore the press of his thigh against hers. Lifting one hand, she patted her hair. She'd released it from its braid for the evening, clipping it away from her face with a pair of tortoiseshell combs.

"Considerate is not something you've accused me of being in the past, Cassie."

She shrugged. "Didn't you say something the other day about turning over a new leaf?" Half of her wanted to edge away from him. The other half wanted to move nearer. She settled for staying exactly where she was.

"So I did," Brand acknowledged. He took a moment to pour a bit more wine for himself and Cassie. "Speaking of new things." He indicated the striking apricot linen ensemble she had one. "I take it your shopping expedition this afternoon was a success?"

"I got a little carried away," Cassie confessed.

In truth, she'd gone on a spending spree.

It had started with the purchase of a beautifully simple cream silk dress she'd spotted in the window of a boutique. No fuss. No flourishes. Just a remarkably flattering garment that struck her as absolutely perfect for a Saturday evening dinner party in Palm Springs. A foray into another shop had produced a dainty pair of matching cream sandals and a fragile little evening purse. She'd mentally accessorized the outfit with her mother's exquisite emerald drop earrings and matching pendant and been thrilled.

From there, Cassie had impulsively picked out and tried on an armful of casually classic sportswear and an assortment of separates that seemed suitable for work. She'd ended up buying nearly everything, plus a shopping bag full of accessories. Finally, after years of purchasing plain cotton underwear, she'd even allowed herself to be tempted into splurging on some very luxurious lingerie.

"Maybe you should do that more often," Brand remarked.

Cassie had taken another bit of pizza. She paused to clear her mouth. "What? Go shopping?"

"No." He took a sip of wine. "Get carried away."

"O-oh." She had trouble getting the single syllable out of her throat.

Brand put down his wineglass with a slow, deliberate movement. Then he turned toward her. After a moment, he reached forward and brushed the ball of his right thumb gently along the curving line of her lower lip.

"Pizza sauce," he murmured in explanation as he broke the contact. Cassie saw that there was, indeed, a small red smear on his thumb. A quiver ran through her as she watched him lick it off.

She shifted involuntarily, conscious of the provocative sensations his brief touch had stirred in her body. Her mouth felt warm and tender, like a piece of fruit brought to a perfect degree of ripeness by the sun.

"I have a napkin," she told him in a husky voice. Her pulse was racing and she was aware of the press of her breasts against the wispy constraint of the new satin-and-lace bra she was wearing.

"I know that."

The banquette seemed to be getting smaller by the second. Cassie could feel herself responding to the utter maleness of the man who was sitting next to her. The subtle tang of Brand's cologne tantalized her nostrils. She gazed at his face, unable to look away.

His eyes.

Blue seemed such an inadequate adjective to describe their complex, compelling color. Cassie could make out flecks of gray embedded like shards of silver in the rich lapis lazuli depths. She found herself fascinated by the way his irises darkened to navy at the rims.

Cassie ran the tip of her tongue across her lower lip. For an instant, she was sure she could taste the flavor of Brand's skin on the spot where he'd touched her.

His mouth.

She could remember, with every fiber of her being, how his mouth had felt against hers three weeks before. The heat. The hunger. The heady promise of much, much more. They had all been part of the devouring demanding kiss that had held her in such helpless thrall.

What was happening now was not a matter of her picking up cues from Brand. It wasn't a matter of pretending for the sake of *Prodigal* or anything else, either. No, the emotions she was experiencing in this moment were very real—and they were threatening to overwhelm her.

Cassie inhaled shakily, a small portion of her brain registering amazement that she still knew how to breathe properly. She felt herself teetering on the brink of a momentous discovery. She felt unsafe. Unsure. She also felt more excited than she could ever remember feeling in her life.

"Brand—"

"Cassie—"

She thought she could see a reflection of her own internal tumult in Brand's expression—a hint that he shared whatever it was she was going through. Her fingers itched to touch him. She ached to trace the strong lines of his face, to stroke the thickness of his hair. And she knew—she absolutely knew—that she wanted him to touch her, too.

But then, without warning, Brand's gaze flicked sideways. His expression changed radically. An instant later, Cassie understood why.

"Well, well. Hello, Cassie Addams."

A few simple words drawled in a raspy world-famous voice. Cassie felt those simple words shatter the intimacy that had sprung up between her and Brand the way a brick would shatter a plate-glass window.

No, she wanted to cry aloud. Not now!

Cassie clenched her hands in frustration, letting her short unpolished nails bite into her palms. Reluctantly she turned to her right to confront the source of this very unwanted interruption.

"Hello, Chet," she said stiffly.

A rather suggestive smile rearranged Chet Walker's jaded features.

"It's been a while," he remarked, his dark brown eyes roving over her with open interest. "You're looking good, babe. Really good. Even better than I remembered."

Cassie felt as though she was standing in the middle of a mine field with no choice but to march forward. She didn't dare glance at Brand, although she was aware he'd gone very still. In a matter of seconds, all his beliefs about her supposed involvement with Chet Walker—beliefs she'd deliberately let stand—would either be reinforced or revealed as totally wrong. She didn't know which eventuality would be worse.

"You're looking pretty much the same, Chet," she replied, taking in the tight leather pants and partially unbuttoned silk shirt he was wearing.

"Oh, yeah?" he responded with a toss of his tangled sun-gilded hair. "And here I was hoping you'd think I'd improved."

There was a brief pause. Cassie saw Chet's gaze move from her to Brand and back again. One corner of his mouth curled knowingly.

"So," he went on in a faintly baiting manner, "the stories about you and your boss are true, huh?"

"That depends on what stories you're talking about," Brand replied with cool precision, speaking up for the first time. His manner was intimidatingly assured as he extended his hand to the younger man. "I'm Brand Marcus."

Chet eyed Brand warily. The actor had a reputation as a brawler, but Cassie had the impression that he was more a bully boy than a fighter. "Yeah, right," he said slowly after several seconds. Extending his own hand, he clasped Brand's and shook it briefly. "Chet Walker."

"I know," Brand responded. "I've seen your pictures."

"I've seen yours, too." Chet rubbed his stubbled chin with one hand and glanced at Cassie again. "I, ah, admire your taste, man. If you don't mind me saying so."

"I don't." As he spoke, Brand brought his right arm up in a smooth movement and rested it along the back of the banquette. Cassie felt the caressing pressure of his fingers as they curved to follow the line of her shoulder. The gesture was pointedly possessive. "I've admired yours on occasion, as well."

Chet laughed. It wasn't a particularly pleasant sound. Cassie shifted uncomfortably, then went still as Brand's fingers tightened against her flesh. She had the feeling she was caught between two circling adversaries. She wanted to say or do something, but she was afraid of aggravating the situation. Finally she cleared her throat and spoke.

"Are you alone tonight, Chet?" she asked.

The actor's brows shot up. "Is that an invitation, babe? Or a hint you want me to leave?"

Cassie glanced sideways at Brand. His expression was bland to the point of boredom, but there was a rigidity in the set of his jaw that sent a prickle of apprehension dancing up her spine. She looked back at Chet.

"It's neither," she informed him tartly. "It's a simple, straightforward question."

Chet made a halfhearted gesture of conciliation. "Okay. Okay. I'll give you a simple, straightforward answer. No, I'm not alone. Why should I be when there's so much company available? I'm with the blond fox over there." Her jerked his thumb toward the far end of the restaurant. "Her name's Mallory," he went on. "Ah, no. *Valerie*. Yeah. That's it. Valerie Thom-something. I call her Honey. She's an aspiring actress, but she aspires a lot better than she acts, if you know what I mean." He paused, as though waiting for a reaction. When he got none, he shrugged indifferently, then turned his attention back to Cassie. "Anyway, like I said before, babe, you're looking good. Maybe I'll see you 'round."

Cassie nodded.

"Well, gotta go," the actor announced flatly. That said, he turned on his heel and swaggered away.

Neither Cassie nor Brand spoke for at least two minutes. Cassie kept her head bent slightly. She picked up her fork and prodded her slice of pizza several times. Then she realized she wasn't hungry and put the eating utensil down. Her hand was trembling.

Lies on top of lies on top of lies, she reflected miserably. The burden of deception was becoming heavier with each passing moment.

"You obviously made quite an impression on him," Brand remarked abruptly.

"What?" Cassie's head came up with a jerk. Distracted gray-green eyes collided with frigid blue ones. Cassie felt her stomach knot as she saw Brand's eyes. They were smoldering like dry ice. Frighteningly cold, yet capable of burning.

Brand refilled his glass. A few drops of the ruby-red wine spilled on the white linen tablecloth. He set down the nearly empty wine bottle with a thud.

"I said, you obviously made quite an impression on Chet Walker," he repeated. He picked up his glass and half drained it in a single gulping swallow.

"I don't understand, Brand."

"No?" he shot back. He finished his wine and put the glass down. Cassie saw his fingers tighten around the slender stem. She expected to hear the sound of snapping crystal. "He couldn't recall the name of the woman he's with tonight. But he sure as hell remembered who you are!"

Cassie stared at him. A small vein was throbbing dangerously in his right temple and there were whitened indentations at both corners of his mouth.

Brand plainly was on the verge of losing his temper with her. But why? What had she done? It hadn't been her fault Chet Walker had intruded on them!

Cassie suddenly decided it was time to tell Brand the truth. She wondered how he'd react when she voiced her suspicion that the main reason Chet remembered her so well was that she probably was the only woman in Hollywood who'd turned down an invitation to join him in bed.

Cassie moistened her lips. "Brand," she began, struggling to speak steadily, "about Chet and me—"

"No."

"W-what?" she stammered.

"I don't want to hear about it," Brand said, his voice low and harsh.

"But—"

"No!" The single syllable came out with savage intensity. "I do not want to hear about you and Chet Walker. Not now. Not later. Not ever." Brand took a deep breath, then expelled it on a hiss. "Do you understand, Cassie?" he demanded.

Cassie nodded, knowing full well that the slow up-down movement of her head was a lie.

She *didn't* understand. She didn't understand then, and she didn't understand many hours later as she relived the scene in the restaurant over and over again as she tossed and turned in her bed, unable to get to sleep.

The only thing Cassandra Leigh Addams did understand was that something was happening to her. She didn't know what it was. But every instinct she had told her that it was irrevocably linked to Brand and that it was beyond her control.

Chapter Eight

Ladies and gentlemen, we have begun our final descent into Palm Springs,'' a mellifluous-voiced flight attendant announced over the plane's public-address system. ''Please restore your seats and tray tables to their upright and locked positions and be sure your seat belts are securely fastened.''

Cassie closed the cinematography magazine she'd been pretending to read and sat up straight. Sighing, she fiddled restlessly with the skirt of the peach knit T-shirt dress she was wearing. She then raised her hand and fussed with her hair, which she'd braided and pinned into a coil at the nape of her neck.

''You look fine,'' Brand told her quietly.

Cassie froze for a moment, then turned slowly to her right. The three words Brand had just said were the first he'd spoken to her since they'd left the ground in Los Angeles.

Not, she had to admit, that she'd given him any encouragement to make conversation during the trip. She'd boarded the plane laden with far more reading material than she needed for the forty minute flight, and she'd started flipping pages the moment she'd buckled her seat belt.

Cassie knew, deep down, that her ostentatious show of engrossment hadn't deceived Brand for a moment. Yet he'd gone along with her ploy and left her alone.

Alone, but certainly not at peace.

"I don't feel fine," she said frankly after a few seconds.

"Nervous?"

"Aren't you?"

"We've done well so far."

"In other words, no one's realized we've been lying."

Brand's features tightened. "People see what they want to see," he answered, studying her with disconcerting directness.

Cassie shifted under the intensity of his gaze. For one wild instant, she allowed herself to wonder what Brand wanted to see when he looked at her the way he was looking at her now.

"Cassie?"

Cassie realized with a shock that her instant of speculation had stretched into ten or fifteen seconds of very obvious silence.

"I'm all right, Brand," she said hastily. "Everything's all right. Really. Everything." Cassie knew she probably sounded like a tape recording running on fast forward, but she was afraid to stop talking. "I'm just suffering from a touch of—of—stage fright, that's all."

"Maybe I have something that will help calm your nerves."

Cassie stiffened. Coming from almost anyone else, she would have expected this statement to be followed by an offer of a tranquilizer or something stronger. But Brand was adamantly antidrugs. He didn't use them; he had no tolerance for those who did.

She watched as Brand reached into one of the pockets of the dark blue blazer he was wearing. He extracted a small velvet-covered box and wordlessly offered it to her on his open palm.

She knew what it was, of course. Only one thing came in that kind of box. Only one thing.

"Open it, Cassie," Brand said quietly.

I'm not much of an actress, you know, she'd warned him when she'd agreed to go through with this deception.

You don't have to be, he'd responded. *Just take your cues from me.*

Cassie took the box from Brand and pressed the tiny catch on the base of it. The top popped open with a mechanical click.

She gasped.

Nestled inside the satin-lined box was the most exquisite ring she'd ever seen. The main stone was a flawless square-cut emerald that flashed a mesmerizing, mysterious green fire. It was flanked by a pair of icily brilliant diamond baguettes.

She tried to say Brand's name several times. She opened her mouth and moved her lips, but no sound came out. She was dimly aware that the hand she was holding the jeweler's box with was trembling.

"After that item in Telling All, I thought we should make it official," Brand observed. His voice seemed to be reaching her across a great distance. "Let me put it on for you." He took the box from her, removed the ring, then repocketed the box.

Cassie felt him clasp her left hand with his own. She looked down, registering the contrast between his strong, tanned fingers and her paler, more delicate ones. She watched Brand slide the ring into place. Slowly. Deliberately. As though the gesture truly meant something.

The ring fit as though it had been made for her.

Cassie blinked against a sudden pricking of tears. Her vision blurred and she felt her throat close up. She bowed her head. No, she thought desperately, trying to ward off the revelation that had just come to her. Oh, please. No.

Brand hooked two fingers beneath her chin. Using gentle but inexorable pressure, he forced her to look at him. "Cassie? What's wrong?"

"Nothing's wrong," she said instantly.

"Then why are you—" Brand broke off as the plane touched down on the airport runway with a sudden jolt. His grip on her slackened for just an instant, but it was enough to allow Cassie to pull free.

"Nothing's wrong," she repeated, cradling her left hand with her right. She conjured up a smile and saw Brand's eyes narrow and darken in response to it.

"Cassie?" He invoked her name in a tone she'd never heard him use before.

"The ring is beautiful, Brand," she told him steadily, forcing herself to ignore the surge of yearning his voice released within her. "It's perfect."

The first half of this statement was true. The second half was just the opposite and Cassie was achingly aware of it. How could the embodiment of a falsehood be perfect? And that was exactly what the emerald-and-diamond engagement ring was. It was an extravagant prop in an elaborate deception. It was a lie.

With all her heart, Cassie wished this were not so.

She wished it because she was in love with Brand Marcus.

She was in love with him, and she would have given anything to be able to believe that the ring he had placed on her finger so carefully was a symbol that he loved her, too.

What am I going to do? Cassie asked herself for the dozenth time.

It was a few minutes after six in the evening and she was sitting on the terrace of the Wyatts' lovely Mediterranean-style house, staring at the turquoise-tiled swimming pool below. Sheila Parker was stretched out on a chaise longue to her left, sipping a glass of wine. Every now and again,

Cassie caught a whiff of the other woman's subtly provocative perfume.

She couldn't help comparing that richly sensual scent with the light floral cologne she was wearing. In fact, she couldn't help comparing a lot of things about Sheila with a lot of things about herself.

Cassie adjusted her position and glanced toward the house, wondering uneasily where Graham and Brand were. They'd excused themselves about a half hour before, ostensibly to go inside and look at a recent addition to Graham's extensive collection of southwestern art. While the two men had been chatting pleasantly as they'd made their exit, Cassie had sensed a great deal of tension swirling beneath their surface congeniality.

At least, she'd *thought* she'd sensed it. Cassie was very much aware that she was filtering everything around her through the clouded screen of her turbulent emotions. She was at the point where each word she heard, each gesture she saw, seemed freighted with deep and disturbing significance.

There had been the brief but potent smile she'd seen Brand flash at Sheila as he'd gotten up to follow Graham off the terrace. Cassie knew there'd been a message in that smile. A message that, judging by the way she inclined her fair head, Sheila had received and understood.

Exactly what had the nonverbal exchange meant? Cassie didn't know.

Nor did she know the meaning of the look Brand had given her just before he'd made his way into the house. What she did know is that the expression in his eyes had made her feel as though the air around her had been charged by a lightning strike. The atmosphere had seemed to quiver with electricity.

Cassie bit her lip, squeezed her eyes shut and prayed for the strength to endure the ordeal ahead. Somehow she'd made it through the past five hours without betraying the devastating discovery she'd made about herself and her true feelings for Brand. But it hurt. Dear Lord, it hurt so much!

Cassie came out of her painful reverie with a start, suddenly registering the fact that Sheila Parker was speaking to her. She opened her eyes and straightened up in her seat.

"I—I'm sorry, Sheila," she said awkwardly. "I'm afraid I wasn't listening."

"I wasn't really saying anything important," Sheila replied reassuringly. Her melodious voice held a hint of magnolia drawl. "I was just remarking that I used to fiddle with my engagement ring, too." She fluttered the beautifully manicured fingers of her left hand, displaying a large marquise-cut diamond set in platinum.

Taken aback, Cassie glanced down and realized that she had, indeed, been "fiddling" with the emerald-and-diamond ring Brand had given her so unexpectedly. In fact, she'd unwittingly rotated it 180 degrees. It now looked as though she was wearing a wedding band.

"Oops," she said with a shaky laugh. She quickly readjusted the ring. The green and crystalline stones winked at her mockingly.

"It's a beautiful ring," Sheila commented.

Cassie looked at her. "Yes," she agreed after a moment. "Yes, it is."

"Did you and Brand pick it out together?"

Cassie shook her head. "No. He, ah, surprised me with it."

"Really?" Sheila seemed more than casually interested. "Graham did the same thing with mine. Unfortunately it was a size too small. I could barely get it over the first knuckle of my ring finger." She smiled suddenly, her long-lashed brown eyes growing luminous. "But I didn't care. It's the thought that counts, right?"

Her words flicked Cassie on the raw. She flinched inwardly. "Right" was all she could say.

Sheila pulled a droll face. "Graham and I had a terrible fight about getting it enlarged. I was terrified he'd change his mind if I took it off. Eventually I gave in, of course. I think the reason I fiddled with it so much once I got it back was that I needed to keep reassuring myself that it was real and that Graham genuinely wanted to marry me."

"I'm not used to wearing very much jewelry," Cassie improvised lamely, looking toward the swimming pool. "And Brand's ring is... well, I haven't had it very long. I mean, he and I have been... together for some time. And we've known we wanted to get married." She forced herself to face Sheila again. "But in the beginning, we tried to...to keep things to ourselves."

"I wish Graham and I had been able to do that," Sheila declared with an odd degree of intensity. "What happened between us happened so quickly. And so publicly! Even now, well, I know you understand, Cassie. Aren't there times when you feel as though it's all make-believe? Times when you wonder whether what you and Brand are doing is for each other or for an audience?"

Cassie said nothing. Even if she'd been able to find the words to respond to Sheila's questions, she doubted she'd be able to voice them.

Sheila frowned suddenly. "I don't suppose any of this is easy for you, is it," she mused.

Cassie caught her breath. Dear Lord. Did Sheila know?

She cleared her throat, then said very carefully, "I don't suppose it's easy for you, either, Sheila."

Cassie wasn't certain what reaction she expected from Sheila. But certainly she hadn't expected to see the other woman's beautiful eyes cloud with distress while her face turned pale beneath its honey-gold tan.

"No," Brand's former lover said in a tight voice. "It's not."

Graham and Brand came back out onto the terrace a few minutes later. Most of the tension Cassie thought she'd detected between them before seemed to be gone. There was still a hint of rivalry—a certain jockeying for advantage. But she sensed this was a matter of masculine instinct rather than the product of personal animosity.

It quickly became apparent that Graham had resolved his reservations about doing *Prodigal*. Indeed, he made it abundantly clear that he was extremely eager to take on the part of Dan Farlow. Sheila, once again serene, was swift to contribute several very perceptive comments about the role of Sally Harper.

Brand's satisfaction with the situation was palpable. Cassie could sense him weighing each word of the character interpretations Graham and Sheila were offering. She watched him nod sharply, gesture decisively. She heard him communicate his views about Dan and Sally in a few incisive phrases. She realized he was already directing the film inside his head.

Cassie had seen Brand this way before. Involved. Engrossed. She now understood that the passionate intensity he brought to his work was one of the many things she loved about him.

She couldn't stop herself from wondering what it would be like if he brought that same passionate intensity to a relationship with a woman.

To a relationship with her.

Cassie closed her eyes.

"No, no, Sheila," she heard Graham growl in his distinctive velvet-gravel voice. The actor had gained some weight and lost some hair in the years since he'd first burst onto the public scene, but his voice was more compelling than it had ever been. "Dan Farlow would never do that."

"Why not?" Sheila challenged. "He wants Sally to know how he feels."

"No, he doesn't. Because at that point in the story the main thing he feels is fear."

"But he's in love with her, Graham. He's in love with Sally Harper and he knows it."

"And that's why he's afraid."

Brand.

Cassie lost track of what Graham and Sheila were saying. The sudden thundering of her pulse drowned out their words.

Brand had crossed to where she was sitting. Cassie could feel him standing next to her. She quivered with an elemental awareness of his proximity from the crown of her head to the soles of her feet.

"Cassie."

She opened her eyes and looked up at him. His expression was solemn and serious. His sky-colored gaze was steady.

For a moment, Cassie thought Brand intended to kiss her. Her lips parted on a quick rush of breath. She lifted her chin a little.

But Brand didn't kiss her. Instead he stroked the tips of his fingers down her cheek and over the satin fullness of her mouth. "Thank you," he murmured.

Then Sheila said his name and asked a question. After a fractional hesitation, he withdrew his hand and turned to answer her, leaving Cassie bereft.

The rest of the evening was dominated by talk about *Prodigal*. For this, Cassie was grateful. The more absorbed Brand, Graham and Sheila were in the film, the less attention they were likely to pay to her. And the less attention they paid to her, the better her chances of carrying off what had become a deception within a deception.

She didn't have to pretend she was in love with Brand. She was. But she couldn't let him know that. She had to make him believe she was making believe for the sake of the movie, just as he was. She had to disguise her true feelings while playing her part in a sham romance that she desperately wanted to be real.

She told herself over and over again she could do it because she had no other choice. She'd committed herself and there was no turning back without destroying everything.

Then Cassie discovered that Sheila had put her and Brand in the same bedroom.

"Look, sweetheart—"

Something inside Cassie recoiled from the endearment. "Don't call me that, Brand," she said tautly.

"What?"

"Don't . . . call me . . . sweetheart."

Brand raked his fingers back through his hair in a gesture Cassie was aware indicated that he was running out of patience. She didn't care. She was in no mood to heed it, nor any other warning signals about the chancy state of her pseudofiancé's temper.

"I've been calling you 'sweetheart' for more than three weeks," he reminded her.

"In public," she returned fiercely. "*Not* in private. You can call me that when we have an audience. But not when it's just the two of us. Do you understand?"

"No, dammit, I don't understand!" Brand answered harshly. He took a step forward. Cassie instantly, almost involuntarily, took a step back. She saw his entire body go rigid. The muscles of his jaw knotted.

They were standing in the center of the spacious guest suite Sheila Parker had ushered Cassie into about forty minutes before. Graham Wyatt had been the one to suggest that Cassie might like to retire for the evening after he'd caught her yawning into her hand for the third time. Brand had swiftly seconded the idea.

Why hadn't she anticipated the sleeping arrangements? Cassie asked herself angrily. How could she so stupidly have assumed that she and Brand would be given separate rooms?

"I've put you in here," Sheila had said with a charming smile as she'd gestured around the second-floor suite. "I hope you find it comfortable."

Cassie had been on the verge of offering a sincere compliment about the decor when she'd realized that there were two suitcases sitting next to the king-size bed opposite the door. One of the suitcases was hers. The other was Brand's.

Had she said anything to Sheila? No! She'd stood there, mute and blushing, while the actress had bade her good-night and left.

Brand had come upstairs about a half hour later. He'd knocked once on the door, then entered the bedroom without waiting for a response.

"Cassie," Brand's voice was more moderate than it had been a minute before, "I don't like this situation any more than you do."

"Really? Well, I don't like it at all!"

"What do you want me to do? Ask for separate bedrooms?"

"Yes."

"And what do I say?" he demanded. "That we're saving ourselves for marriage? May I remind you that we've gone to a great deal of trouble to create the impression that we're lovers?"

"You don't have to remind me of anything, Brand."

"Then what do you want me to—"

"Tell—tell Sheila you snore!" Cassie suggested desperately, then winced at the utter stupidity of the idea.

Brand took a deep breath, then expelled it on a sigh. "She knows I don't, Cassie."

Cassie bit the inside of her lip. The pain she inflicted on the tender flesh was nothing compared with the pain she felt in her heart. Of course Sheila knows Brand doesn't snore, she thought miserably. She was his lover.

"It's a big bed," he said after a brief silence. "It could sleep three or four."

"Well, I have no real way to judge that," Cassie retorted nastily, goaded by an ugly and unfamiliar feeling of jealousy. "I've never been into orgies."

She'd never seen Brand look as angry as he looked in the first few seconds after she finished speaking. A rush of blood darkened the chiseled ledge of his cheekbones, while the skin around his mouth went white. Cassie found herself flinching from the fury in his face.

Then abruptly his expression changed. "Are you afraid of me, Cassie?" he asked slowly.

Cassie stared at him, stunned. "What?"

Brand closed the distance that separated them in two strides, moving with the feral grace of a jungle cat. Before she realized his intention, he caught her by the upper arms. Cassie tried to pull away, but his hold on her was too strong.

"Is that it?" he demanded. "Are you afraid I'll try to take advantage of you?"

The shock of his question and the power of his physical presence made Cassie's head swim. She drew a shaky breath, wondering if she was going to faint.

His fingers tightened to the bruising point. "Is that what you think?"

Somehow Cassie found the ability to speak. "No, Brand," she whispered. "Oh, no."

There was a long silence. Cassie sensed Brand was weighing her answer, measuring the truth it contained.

His grip on her eased by increments. Finally he released her completely and brought his hands down to his sides. "Then what is it?" he asked. "What's wrong?"

"Nothing's wrong," she insisted, repeating the phrase she'd used on the airplane, what now seemed like a lifetime ago. "I'm just tired. Very, very tired."

They ended up sharing the bed. Brand took the right side, Cassie the left. There was plenty of space for at least two other people in the middle.

"You expected this, didn't you, Brand," Cassie said into the darkness, twisting the emerald-and-diamond ring on her left hand around and around on her finger. She knew she should take it off, but somehow she couldn't.

"Yes."

"And you didn't do anything about it."

She heard something ruffle the pattern of his breathing. It might have been a laugh. Then again, it might have been a sigh.

"Actually, I did."

Cassie turned her head, her hair rustling against the embroidered linen pillowcase. There was just enough moonlight filtering in through the sheerly curtained windows to allow her to make out Brand's profile. His eyes were closed.

"What did you do?" she asked.

Cassie saw Brand's dark lashes stir and his eyes open. After a moment, he turned to look at her. The movement left his face virtually obscured by shadows. So close, she thought achingly. He's so close. What would he do if I reached out to him? If I told him how I feel?

"I went out and bought a pair of pajamas," he said.

Chapter Nine

Kisses.

Lips meeting. Matching. Mating. The sinuous slide of tongue against tongue. The taste and texture of a headily familiar male mouth.

Cassie murmured her pleasure.

It was a dream. A dream that made her shiver with sweet anticipation. The impulse had been there, aching and alive, for much longer than she had understood or admitted. But now her conscious control was gone and she was free to surrender to it. She could abandon herself to the fantasy of having what she knew she wanted.

Brand. Always Brand.

Caresses.

Hands touching. Teasing. Tempting. The sensual stroke of skin against skin. The passionately possessive glide of a man's hard palm over a woman's soft flesh.

Cassie moaned her need.

It was a dream. A dream that made her burn with honeyed fire. She had never fully realized the power of her imagination. She had never truly recognized the wildness she had leashed within her, waiting to defy the twin restraints of inhibition and insecurity.

Brand. Ever and always Brand.

The shimmering warmth of his breath against her cheek. The exquisite nip of his teeth at her earlobe. The evocative tense and release of the sleek muscles of his shoulders and back beneath her hands.

They all seemed so utterly real to Cassie. So absolutely right.

"Cassie."

The shocking sound of Brand's voice. The sudden clutch of his fingers.

These, too, seemed utterly real to Cassie. Utterly real, and absolutely wrong.

And then she knew. *This was no dream.*

Slowly, ever so slowly, Cassie opened her eyes and looked up into Brand's face. She blinked once or twice, her mind vaguely registering that it must be morning because the room was filled with the golden haze of daylight.

Brand repeated her name in a gut-wrenching tone. Emotions Cassie didn't want to see—much less accept as being real—shadowed his eyes, darkening them to a depthless midnight. He was very pale. She felt a convulsive shudder rack his taut body.

"I thought I was dreaming," he said hoarsely. "Dear God. Cassie. I thought it was a dream."

With that, he released his hold on her and abruptly rolled away. A moment later, he sat up. His brow was damp with perspiration, his lips were compressed into a rigid white line. His chest heaved and his nostrils flared with the disordered force of his breathing.

Cassie levered herself up and reached out toward him with her left hand. The emerald on her ring finger caught a shaft of sunlight.

She had to make Brand understand that he—that *they*—had done nothing wrong. She had to make him understand that she wanted him. That she needed him. That she loved him!

Cassie touched him with the tips of her fingers. Brand reacted to the contact as though it seared his skin and burned straight through to the bone. Casting aside the sheet that covered the lower half of his body, he swung his legs off the side of the mattress and got out of bed.

"Brand?" She was barely able to force his name out of her throat.

Brand wouldn't—or couldn't—look at her. "I'm sorry, Cassie," he said harshly, then stalked off into the bathroom that was part of the lavish guest suite. He moved swiftly, as though he couldn't get away from her fast enough. A few seconds after he shut the door to the bathroom, Cassie heard the liquid gush of the shower.

She began shaking her head back and forth, back and forth. "No," she whispered. "No."

Cassie hadn't known it was possible to ache the way she ached at this moment. Nothing had prepared her for the fevered hunger that seemed to suffuse every cell of her brain and body. She had been lifted partway to heaven and given a glimpse of paradise only to be plunged back to earth by the very man who'd offered her her first intimation of ecstacy. The contrast was too stark, too painful.

Why had he stopped? she cried out inside her head and heart as she searched for answers to questions she'd never expected to ask of herself. Had it been something she'd done? Something she hadn't done?

For the first time in her life, Cassie felt burdened by her physical innocence. She wasn't ignorant, just terribly inexperienced. But she'd always thought, when she'd thought about it at all, that instincts born of love would guide her when the time—and the man—were right.

Had Brand somehow guessed she was a virgin? Had he suddenly realized that his tabloid-based assumptions about her private life must be wrong? Was that why he'd stopped?

Cassie pressed her fingers to her lips, choking back a sob of frustration. She looked at the tightly closed bathroom door, yearning for the man behind it.

Brand had said he'd thought he was dreaming, she recalled. Had he meant dreaming of being with her? Or had his subconscious supplied him with another lover? Had she been the recipient of kisses and caresses he'd wanted to bestow on someone else? Had the shock of discovering that the woman of his dreams was really—

There was a sudden knock on the bedroom door. Cassie started violently, her heart leaping within her breast. The questions she'd been asking herself collided with one another, burying her ability to think clearly beneath a pile of emotional wreckage.

A second knock. This one much more forceful than the first.

"J-just a... m-minute," Cassie called shakily. Looking down, she realized that the straps of her nightgown had slipped off her shoulders. The lace-trimmed neckline was gaping away from her body, revealing the upper swell of her breasts.

With clumsy fingers, Cassie tried to tug the garment back into place as she got out of bed. She then stumbled across the floor to answer the rapping summons. She was dimly aware that the shower had been turned off.

Cassie had some vague notion that it must be Sheila or Graham doing the knocking. The shock of finding out who it actually was nearly made her pass out.

"Uncle Jordan!" she gasped, staring at the tall balding man who was standing before her. She grabbed for the doorjamb with her right hand and clutched at the top of her nightgown with her left. "What are you doing here?"

"What am I doing here?" Jordan Addams repeated. His penetrating steel-gray eyes fixed briefly on the emerald on her left hand, then lifted to her face. "What do you think I'm doing here, Cassie? I finished my business in New York sooner than I expected, so I flew back to L.A. last night. I figured it was time you and I had a face-to-face talk. Then I found out you weren't in L.A. You're off in Palm Springs with Brand Marcus visiting my good friend, Graham Wyatt. So I called and asked if it would be all right if I dropped by to surprise you. That's when I heard—"

He broke off suddenly and focused on a spot behind Cassie. His face turned an alarming shade of puce. His expression was very similar to the one he'd worn nearly eight years before, when he'd caught one of the guests at her sweet sixteen party trying to give her more than a birthday kiss. That episode had precipitated his unilateral decision that she should finish her high-school career at a private girls' academy in Switzerland.

Quivering with a sense of impending disaster, Cassie slowly turned in the direction her uncle was staring.

She knew she was going to see Brand again and she tried to brace for it. Unfortunately she failed to prepare herself for the possibility that Brand would be wearing nothing but a towel. The white terry-cloth oblong he had knotted around his hips was big enough to cover the essentials and that was about it.

Brand obviously had not bothered to use the towel before wrapping it around himself and stepping out of the bathroom. His lean, tanned body was still damp. Drops of water spangled the inverted triangle of hair on his broad chest like silver beads. One drop broke free and ran a provocative course down his torso into the shadowed indentation of his navel.

Cassie caught her lower lip between her teeth, trying to ignore the wave of bone-melting heat that surged through her. Her eyes met Brand's. Her pulse scrambled. The walls of the bedroom seemed to shrink inward.

Jordan Addams cleared his throat with an angry rumble. Brand's gaze shifted. Cassie saw him draw himself up, as though he was responding to an unspoken challenge. Turning her head, she glanced back at her uncle.

"Get dressed," he ordered with grim precision. "You're getting married."

Cassie stood in the doorway of the guest suite bathroom, staring at Brand's back. He was in front of the sink, head bent, hands gripping the edge of the tiled countertop. The sleek muscles of his shoulders were taut; his spine was stiff. He was still clad in nothing but the white towel.

"Have you lost your mind?" Cassie was trembling with anger, confusion and a desperate kind of hurt.

Her uncle had exited the scene a few moments before, departing to make what he'd trenchantly termed "the necessary arrangements." Cassie had had the near-hysterical urge to inquire whether those arrangements would include arming himself with a loaded shotgun. She'd choked back the question, however, just as she'd choked back so many other things during the previous five minutes.

She had no intention of choking back anything now.

"I don't think so," Brand answered as he turned on the faucet. Although quiet, his voice carried clearly through the sound of the running water. "Why do you ask?"

Brand had pivoted on his heel, walked into the bathroom and closed the door as soon as Jordan Addams had left the bedroom. Cassie had been too stunned by the events of the previous five minutes to immediately react. Once she'd finally recovered the ability to move, she'd followed him. She'd flung open the bathroom door without the slightest hesitation, driven past the point of caring about what she might see.

"Why do I ask? Brand, at this very moment, my uncle is downstairs making reservations for us to fly to Las Vegas to get married!"

Brand bent and splashed some water on his face, then turned off the faucet. "Yes," he said without inflection, reaching for one of the small monogrammed towels on the countertop. "I know."

"Why aren't you stopping him?"

Brand's head came up suddenly. Blue eyes met hazel ones in the large mirror above the sink. "Why aren't you?"

Because I want to marry you.

For one terrifying moment, Cassie was certain she'd spoken the thought aloud. Only Brand's lack of reaction assured her that she hadn't. She took an unsteady step backward, watching as he dried his face, discarded the towel, then slowly turned around.

"What do you want me to do?" he asked. "Tell Jordan the truth?"

"I—"

"I could do it," Brand went on evenly. "I could tell him our engagement is a sham. And I could tell him I've been using you to make sure *Prodigal* gets made the way I want it made."

Cassie wanted to cry out in protest at this last sentence, but she managed to keep still.

"Your uncle knows me pretty well," Brand continued. "I'm sure he'd believe me if I told him those things." His features hardened suddenly and his voice turned rough. "And I'm equally sure he'd call me a liar if I told him we shared a bed last night and didn't make love."

"But we didn't!"

"We came damned close."

A sudden wave of sensual memories threatened to swamp Cassie. Her breath unraveled in her throat and her body started to melt. She tried to steel herself against the sensations sluicing through her. "And...and that's why you're letting my uncle force you into—" She faltered.

"Your uncle isn't forcing me into anything!"

Cassie stared at him, unable to hide her bewilderment. None of this made any sense to her! "You're saying you *want* to—to—" The muscles of her throat tightened like a noose and her voice failed her.

"What I want—" Brand broke off abruptly, his naked chest expanding as he sucked in a ragged breath. His eyes blazed like molten sapphires.

Cassie felt her heart skip a beat. "Brand?" she whispered.

The fire raging in the depths of his brilliant eyes was banked down—almost extinguished—in the space of a single heartbeat. When Brand spoke again, the words were calm and controlled.

"If you want me to go downstairs and tell your uncle we aren't flying to Vegas because we're not getting married, I will," he said. "But I'll also have to tell him why."

"You mean, tell him the truth."

Brand nodded.

Cassie swallowed. "Then Graham Wyatt would find out that we aren't really..." She made a weak little gesture.

Another nod.

"And he wouldn't do *Prodigal*."

"No, he wouldn't."

Cassie moistened her lips. "The whole project could be ruined."

"Possibly."

"Probably."

Brand shrugged slightly. His features were unreadable, his eyes opaque. Someone who didn't know him would very likely say he was indifferent to the topic being discussed.

But Cassie did know him. She knew him, and "indifferent" was the last word she'd use to describe him at this moment.

She thought about what *Prodigal* meant to Brand.

Then she thought about what Brand meant to her.

He didn't love her. She was painfully aware of that. In fact, given his recent behavior, she wasn't even certain he liked her anymore. Yet she loved him. She didn't know how or when she'd begun to do so; she only knew that she did. She loved him and she'd do anything she could for him.

Anything.

Cassie tried to take a deep, cleansing breath, but her chest felt as though it had been strapped with iron bands. All she could manage was a short, shallow gasp.

"Cassie?" Brand seemed reluctant to say her name.

She squared her slender shoulders and met his gaze. "Let's go to Las Vegas."

Roughly twelve hours later, Cassie sat on the edge of a chair in the lavish bridal suite of one of the most expensive casino-hotels in Las Vegas. She was watching her new husband prowl around the room like a caged animal.

Married.

She and Brand were *married*.

The ceremony had taken place in a small twenty-four-hour wedding chapel. Her uncle had given her away. Graham Wyatt and Sheila Parker had served as witnesses.

Cassie scuffed her feet against the thick pile of the wall-to-wall carpeting and sighed. She toyed with the softly draped skirt of the cream silk dress she was wearing. It was the same cream silk dress she'd purchased during her Rodeo Drive shopping spree just a few days before.

She wasn't certain why she'd insisted on changing into the garment before the ceremony. Perhaps there had been an element of defiance in the act. She also suspected that she'd donned the dress because, deep in the secret recesses of her heart, she'd been trying to live out a fantasy.

Her uncle had told her she looked beautiful. Graham and Sheila had offered similar compliments. Brand had said nothing. He hadn't needed to. Cassie knew her appearance had surprised—even shocked—him. She'd seen the expression in his eyes when she'd walked toward him in the chapel.

She'd seen the same expression in them when he'd released her after brushing his mouth lightly over hers at the close of the wedding ceremony.

Cassie stared down at her left hand. Her third finger now bore a simple gold circlet as well as the emerald engagement ring. She rubbed the smooth metal band with the ball of her thumb.

"I'm sorry," Brand said suddenly.

Cassie brought her head up. "What?"

Brand walked toward her, coming to a stop about two feet away. It was the closest he'd been to her since her uncle, Graham and Sheila had left the two of them alone in the bridal suite about thirty minutes before.

"I'm sorry, Cassie," he repeated quietly. "I never wanted—I never intended things to go this far."

She swallowed. The taste in her mouth was bitter. "I know that."

"Do you?"

"Yes. I do." She gave a rueful little laugh and saw Brand's features tighten. "'I do.' That seems to be the phrase of the day, doesn't it?" She felt herself start to laugh again. She choked the sound back.

"Cassie." Brand took a step forward, his dark brows slanting together in a frown. He reached out as though to touch her.

"No." She shook her head once, then looked away. She didn't know what she'd do if he touched her. She definitely didn't want to find out. "Don't. Not when we're alone."

Brand let his hand drop back to his side. He took a deep breath, then exhaled it very slowly. "All right," he said finally. "Not when we're alone."

There was a long pause. Cassie felt the hot sting of tears in the corners of her eyes. She blinked against them, then drew an unsteady breath.

"Do you . . . do you remember the day we started this?" she asked huskily.

"Yes." An emotion she couldn't identify sharpened Brand's voice. "I remember it."

Cassie turned her head and looked at him. "I had lunch with Noreen that day. She said she'd always wondered how far you'd go to make sure a movie got done the way you believed it should be. It's too bad we can't tell her."

Chapter Ten

Cassie, are you listening to me?'' Lee Allen demanded.

Cassie pressed the knuckles of her left hand against her brow and continued scribbling notes on a pad with her right. Ten days had passed since she and Brand had exchanged wedding vows in Las Vegas. By some miracle, they'd gotten back to Los Angeles before word of their elopement had leaked out. Brand had personally announced their marriage—and the signing of Graham Wyatt and Sheila Parker for *Prodigal*—to Marcus Moviemaking staffers. He'd also dictated a pair of news releases and had them distributed to the press.

''Cassie?'' The phone line crackled with static.

''Yes, Lee,'' she answered tightly, bringing her left hand down from her throbbing temples. ''I'm listening. The owner of the motel where we'll be staying reminds you of Norman Bates in *Psycho*.''

''Right. Only female. At least, I *think* Eula Mae Bertram is female. But never mind. You'll find out soon enough. You and Brand still set to fly in tomorrow afternoon?''

"Um . . . y-yes." Cassie tried to control the tremor in her voice. She realized she was fiddling with the rings on her left hand again. She forced herself to stop.

"Did I tell you how much I appreciate you two getting married?"

The throbbing in her skull erupted into a hammer-and-anvil pounding. "No," Cassie managed to reply.

"What's that, Cassie? This is a lousy connection."

"No, Lee," she repeated more strongly. "No, you didn't."

"You've heard about the problem Miss Bertram has with show biz people."

"Yes."

"She reads all the tabloids, you know. And she believes every word. She got real uptight when she saw the stories about you and Brand. She told me she didn't want people living in sin in her motel. She was set to cause a major stink."

"Oh."

"Yeah. I can hardly wait until she figures out about Freddie and Francis, the guys from makeup. They're on the list to stay at her place, too. But she's squared away as far as you and Brand go. Once she heard about your elopement, she wanted to put you in the Bide-a-While's bridal suite."

Cassie felt herself pale. "Lee, you didn't—"

"No, no" came the quick reassurance. "Brand made it crystal clear he wants two adjoining rooms. One for an office, one for . . ." Lee paused, then finished with unusual delicacy, "Well, whatever."

"Good. Thank you."

"Just doing my job. But, uh, you should know—it's not going to be honeymoon heaven."

Cassie suppressed a sigh. She'd spent the past eight nights ensconced in the spare bedroom of Brand's Malibu beach house. That hadn't been honeymoon heaven, either. But she'd gotten through it. And she'd get through the next two months on location, too. Somehow.

"I'm not expecting the Ritz, Lee."

"I know you're not. You wouldn't complain even if you were. You're a trouper, Cassie."

The compliment surprised and touched her. "Thank you," she responded.

"You're welcome." The sound of a throat being cleared rumbled through the line. "Well, I guess that's about it from— Oh, no. Wait. There're two other things you'd better know about Eula Mae. Number one, she's a real shutterbug. She loves sneaking up and taking pictures of people. Number two, she's a busybody. And, uh, well...she's probably going to ask you if you got married because you're pregnant."

Cassie closed her eyes and thought about some of the questions and comments she'd heard during the past week and a half. "She won't be the first, Lee," she said softly.

Noreen Krebs appeared in the doorway of Cassie's work space about an hour later. She was carrying a box wrapped in white tissue paper and tied with silver ribbons.

"Hi," she said.

"Hi," Cassie responded with a tentative smile. Her relationship with the older woman had been decidedly off kilter since she'd returned from Las Vegas. "Please. Come in."

Noreen moved from the door to the desk. She extended the parcel. "This is for you. It's an after-the-fact wedding present."

Cassie took the rectangular package. Her hands shook slightly as she set it down in front of her. "Oh, Noreen. You really shouldn't have."

The office manager grimaced. "No kidding, I shouldn't have," she returned with familiar acerbity. "You've pretty much cost me my reputation for knowing everything that goes on around here, you realize."

Cassie gave an unsteady laugh. "I'm sorry."

Noreen made a gesture of dismissal. "No. Don't apologize. I had a feeling that— Well, never mind. I understand."

Dropping her eyes, Cassie fingered one of the long strands of ribbon on the box. She considered Noreen's last two words and what they might imply. After a pause, she said, "I'm not pregnant, Noreen."

"I never thought you were!'

Startled by the vehemence of this statement, Cassie looked up. There was no doubting the affronted sincerity in the older woman's face. "Well, then," she replied carefully, "you're one of the few who doesn't."

"I know you. I know Brand." Noreen punctuated these two assertions by folding her arms. It was plain she did not intend to elaborate.

Several moments passed. Cassie began toying with the ribbons on the package again. She found herself wondering about the "feeling" Noreen had mentioned and few seconds before.

"It's all right with me if you open the box, Cassie." The statement was very dry, very typically Noreen.

Cassie blinked. "Oh, yes." She started to unwrap the package.

"I would have gotten you china, but you neglected to register your pattern."

Cassie peeled the tissue paper back, saying nothing. She stared at the box she'd revealed for a moment, then slowly lifted the lid.

Inside the box was a nightgown and robe of shimmering peach silk. The bodice of the fragile feminine gown and the cuffs and collar of the robe were appliquéd with exquisitely embroidered cream blossoms and pale green leaves.

"Oh," Cassie breathed, torn between an instinctive shock of delight and a nearly overwhelming sense of dismay. "Oh, Noreen."

"I realize it's not the most practical thing to give somebody who's going on location in Texas" came Noreen's embarrassed-sounding response.

Cassie raised her eyes, stroking the fabric of the robe with trembling fingers. She could feel the facade she'd tried so hard to maintain for so many weeks crumbling. "Brand told me you were a romantic," she began tremulously.

"Well, for heaven's sake, don't tell anybody else!" Noreen expostulated, coming around the desk. "It's bad enough that people don't think I'm infallible anymore. But if they find out I'm— Oh, Cassie. No. Don't cry. Do you have any idea what tearstains look like on pure silk?"

Brand came to see Cassie that night.

She'd just gotten into bed after spending two hours packing and repacking her suitcases for Texas when he rapped softly on the door of the room where she'd spent the eight previous nights. It took her a moment to realize what the knocking meant.

"Cassie?" His voice was calm and quiet, blending with the sound of the waves breaking on the beach outside.

"Just—just a second," she responded, sitting up. She couldn't imagine what Brand might want.

Oh, yes, she could. Her heart beat faster at the thought of it and her lips parted on a shuddery sigh. The tips of her breasts tightened beneath the soft cotton of her nightgown.

She'd contemplated the possibility of Brand coming to her countless times during each of the past eight nights. She'd created fantasies so vivid she'd shivered and burned like the victim of a raging fever.

She'd even thought of going to him. If he'd given her the tiniest hint of encouragement, she would have. But he hadn't. While he'd continued to grasp every public opportunity to demonstrate their supposed closeness, he'd been keeping her at arm's length—or farther—whenever they were alone.

"Cassie?"

She swept her hair back over her shoulders with unsteady hands. "Come in," she called.

The door opened. Brand took a step inside, then stopped. He was barefoot and his dark hair was thoroughly mussed. He was wearing jeans and a partially buttoned blue chambray shirt that was untucked on one side.

"I'm sorry," he said after a moment, rubbing his right palm against his thigh. "I didn't realize you were..." His eyes moved over her and he seemed to lose track of what he wanted to say for a second. Then he blinked twice and concluded, "I saw the light under the door."

Cassie tried to smile. She deduced, from the way Brand's brow suddenly furrowed, that her attempt was not very successful. "I just got into bed," she told him, then inclined her head toward the pair of suitcases she'd placed to the left of the door a few minutes before. "I was packing."

"Ah."

"Is there.... Do you want something?"

Brand took another step into the room. Then another. "I wanted to see if you were all right. You seemed upset earlier."

Cassie slid her hands beneath the bedsheets, clenching her fingers. She had not said anything about Noreen's gift or the storm of tears it had triggered. She'd left the gown and robe tucked away in her office. "I'm fine," she replied after a second or two, then looked away.

"Are you sure?" Brand questioned.

She could tell from the proximity of his voice that he'd moved next to the bed. A moment later, she felt the mattress give and knew he'd sat down on the edge of it. She started trembling inside.

"Cassie?" Brand captured her chin gently with his right hand and urged her face back toward his.

Cassie wanted to turn her cheek into his palm, but she steeled herself to resist the urge. She met his eyes and repeated, "I'm fine."

He regarded her intently. The pupils of his eyes seemed to dilate and grow darker. Cassie saw the sudden pulse of a vein in his left temple. He swallowed, the muscles of his throat moving almost convulsively.

Cassie's heart turned a somersault. "What?" she asked.

He didn't say anything.

"Brand?"

Brand let go of her chin. The feel of his fingers lingered on her skin. Cassie watched him take a deep breath, then expel it slowly. His chest rose and fell a second time, then a third.

He looks so tired, Cassie thought painfully. So very tired.

She said his name again. Tentatively. Tenderly.

His eyes slid away from hers for a moment. His features seemed to smooth and solidify, as though he'd suddenly made up his mind about something. He looked back at her, his expression shuttered. "I want you to know," he said slowly, "that I'll make everything right, Cassie. I promise you. I will."

Cassie understood that he was trying to be kind. She also understood that deliberate cruelty would have hurt her less. It was now hideously clear to her that Brand had no idea what she felt . . . or wanted . . . or needed.

Somehow she found the strength to continue looking into his face. She even found the strength to speak in a voice that sounded very close to her own.

"Just make *Prodigal* right," she told him.

Cassie knew, even before the first week of shooting was over, that *Prodigal* was going to be much better than "right." She tried not to be too excited, too expectant. She understood that her judgment was anything but objective and impartial. She was also well aware that there were scores of films that had seemed brilliant on location yet died before they reached the screen.

Still, she *knew*. She absolutely knew. And so, she quickly realized, did nearly everyone associated with the film—including Graham Wyatt.

The time: A few minutes after seven on a summer morning.

The place: The interior of a flyspecked diner that sat forlornly by the highway leading out of a small town in the Texas panhandle.

It was hot. The diner was half-empty. A woman named Sally Harper was serving coffee to a customer she knew would leave her a twenty-five-cent tip if she smiled at him.

Sally's feet hurt, her ugly polyester uniform clung to her in all the wrong places and she had a bacon-grease burn on her left wrist. But she smiled anyway. In her life, every quarter counted.

"Here you go, Virgil," she said with a drawl that was as flat as the landscape outside. "Just the way you like it."

"Cut and print," Brand said in a quiet but carrying voice. Turning his head, he nodded once at the chunky fair-haired man standing to his left. The man was Tim Potter, the assistant director.

Cassie discovered that she'd been holding her breath. She released it on a sigh of satisfaction and smiled to herself. Out of the corner of her eye, she saw two technicians exchange thumbs-up signals.

"Very nice, people. Very nice," Tim Potter called out loudly. "Set for Sheila's close-ups now. Let's snap to."

Cassie stayed where she was, her eyes still on Brand. He seemed aloof from the bustle of activity that had erupted around him, but she knew he was aware of everything and everyone. Even at a distance of twelve or fifteen feet, the force of his concentration was palpable. She saw his gaze shift—assessing, analyzing.

He said something to his assistant director out of the side of his mouth, then moved forward toward Sheila. The actress had wilted against the edge of the scarred Formica counter that dominated the diner. Cassie watched her revive, a lovely smile blossoming on her lips, as Brand approached. She watched Brand smile back, then reach out and place his hands on Sheila's shoulders.

Cassie felt a stab of the destructive emotion that had become unpleasantly familiar to her in recent days. There was no doubting the empathy between Brand and Sheila. She knew attunement between a director and performer was vital but this was more than that.

She hated to see Brand touching the actress. There was nothing sexual or flirtatious in the contact. But she still hated to see it. She particularly hated it since Brand's public displays of affection toward her had dwindled dramatically since they'd arrived in Texas. In an odd way, he seemed to have reverted to treating her the way he'd treated her before they'd embarked on the deception that had so complicated their lives.

So far no one associated with the production appeared to have noticed his aloofness. Certainly no one had said anything about it within her hearing. There were moments when Cassie bleakly wondered whether this was an indication of people's attitudes about marriage. Did the *Prodigal* cast and crew accept the notion that trading "I do's" was the death of romance?

Cassie twisted the rings on her left hand.

"What did that magazine call it?"

The rumbling, reflective voice was Graham Wyatt's. Thoroughly startled, Cassie turned to her right. The actor was standing perhaps a foot behind her, clad in the rumpled suit that was Dan Farlow's costume at the beginning of *Prodigal*.

"Excuse me?" she questioned uncertainly.

"That magazine," he repeated, his brow pleated briefly, then smoothed. "Oh. Yes. 'The Marcus Magic.'"

Cassie saw his eyes shift and focus on what was going on behind her. She felt a prickle of alarm and started trying to think of something distracting to say.

"Directing...writing...producing..." the actor mused. Then, abruptly, his gaze sharpened and he looked directly at Cassie. "I think I would have regretted it until the end of my days if I hadn't decided to do this picture. *Prodigal* is going to be something very special."

He sounded sincere and the expression in his eyes was solemn. But Cassie still felt uneasy. "I think so, too," she answered carefully, then added much less guardedly, "and you're *perfect* as Dan Farlow."

Graham made a self-deprecating gesture. "Given what an imperfect man Dan is, I find that hard to believe. And it's always dangerous to judge a performance based on five days' worth of rushes. Still—" he paused, then chuckled "—I appreciate your assessment. Particularly since you're really the one responsible for this project."

Cassie flushed hotly. Her stomach knotted. He's guessed, she thought, struggling against a wave of panic. He knows!

Despite his agreeing to do *Prodigal*, Cassie had repeatedly wondered whether Graham Wyatt genuinely believed in the supposed relationship between her and Brand. She knew his feelings for his lovely, much-younger wife were very strong, but she also understood how compelling an actor's hunger for a good role was. She couldn't help asking herself whether Graham Wyatt's desire to play Dan Farlow—not his apparent acceptance of her and Brand's deception—had been the reason he'd put aside his concerns about his wife and marriage.

"I don't know what you mean, Graham," she managed to reply.

The actor raised his brows. "You discovered the original property, didn't you?"

"Oh," Cassie said blankly, then blinked. "Oh. *That*."

"Yes, that," Graham affirmed, sounding slightly amused. "I understand from my wife that your husband has been quite eloquent about your cinematic instincts."

His wife. Her husband. Cassie felt more than a little sick. She struggled to keep the distress she was feeling off her face and out of her voice. "Well, I really can't take that much credit."

"Good God, don't let your uncle hear you say that!" Graham interrupted, then grinned roguishly. "It's been my impression that Jordan believes you should always take all the credit you can. And if you can take it above the title—so much the better."

Cassie was surprised into a small laugh. "You know my uncle very well."

"Well enough."

There was a brief pause. Graham loosened the wrinkled tie he was wearing and unbuttoned the top of his rather limp white shirt. Cassie plucked at the front of her cotton T-shirt. They were filming on location in a real diner. Although the place was equipped with several vintage air-conditioning units, they created such an annoying racket that they had to be shut off whenever the cameras were rolling. The temperature on the set was less than comfortable, to say the least. And Cassie knew there was worse to come.

"I don't imagine you're looking forward to shooting exteriors tomorrow," she commented sympathetically to Graham. Her sympathy was real. So was her relief at being able to introduce a neutral topic.

"I can think of more pleasant things than standing out in ninety-degree heat in a suit and tie," the actor acknowledged ruefully. "Then again, it couldn't possibly be as bad as the summer I spent running around some drought-stricken plain in Spain wearing armor."

Cassie understood the reference immediately. *"Saracen Steel."*

Graham gave her a sharp look. "Don't tell me you've seen it! That movie's more than twenty years old."

"Well, so am I," Cassie returned lightly. "I turn twenty-four in a couple of days."

"Oh, yes. Friday, isn't it? I understand the crew is planning a party."

"The crew is desperate for distraction."

"Mmm. It's going to be at your motel, I take it?" Unlike the crew and the rest of the cast, the stars of *Prodigal* were not being lodged in motel rooms. Their contracts specified that a house and housekeeper be supplied for them.

Cassie nodded. "That's only because the Bide-a-While has a pool."

"A desirable commodity in this climate. Do you know, I had a chance meeting with your landlady the other day."

"Did she take your picture?" Cassie asked, curious about his encounter with the proprietress of the Bide-a-While Motel. While Eula Mae Bertram had snapped a few photographs of her, she'd only spoken to her once. And that, as Lee Allen had predicted, had been to inquire whether Brand had married her because he'd gotten her pregnant.

"Oh, yes," Graham responded, chuckling. "I was nearly blinded by those flashbulbs she uses. We also had an, ah, unusual chat. She told me she doesn't hold a very high opinion of a grown man who wears pancake and powder for a living."

"She didn't!"

"Oh, she did. I assure you, she did. She had a few choice words about my wife's appearance, too."

Cassie nodded her understanding. "It's killing Freddie and Francis to make Sheila look so drab, you know. They think it's like vandalizing the *Mona Lisa*. I heard them moaning about it this morning." She frowned for an instant, remembering the tail end of something else she'd heard the two makeup men saying. Something about Sheila not feeling well.

"Well, it is a bit of a shock to see—"

"Cassie!"

The summons was from Brand. The sound of his voice cut effortlessly through the hubbub on the crowded set. Cassie turned in his direction. He'd moved away from Sheila, who was now being fussed over by Freddie. She saw him crook an imperious finger at her. She glanced back at Graham and said, "Excuse me."

"Of course," the actor responded, then gestured her on her way.

Getting to Brand was a bit like running an obstacle course. Cassie had to step over a dozen electrical cables and step around twice that many members of the technical crew and their equipment in order to reach him.

"Yes?" she asked, once she finally arrived at his side.

"Will you see if you can scrounge up some crackers for Sheila?" Brand requested. His voice was husky, almost intimate.

Cassie glanced toward the actress. Sheila had her eyes squeezed shut. There was an aura of weariness about her. It was obvious she was enduring—not enjoying—the ministrations of the makeup man.

Cassie looked inquiringly at Brand. "Is she all right?"

"Fine," he answered, his voice still low. "She's just a little queasy from doing seven takes of the bacon-frying sequence."

The explanation made sense. The fatty smell of the cooking meat had been a bit overpowering, especially in the heat. "Is there anything else I can get her?"

Brand shook his head. A thick comma of dark hair curved down onto his forehead. "No. Thanks."

"Okay." Cassie had a sudden, almost irresistible urge to brush the errant lock of hair back into place. She fought the impulse, giving Brand what she hoped was a neutral smile.

His eyes, which had been the color of a cloudless summer sky, darkened. One corner of his mouth curved up.

For a moment, everything seemed to stand still. It seemed to Cassie that reality began to unravel, that the passage of time slowed and stopped.

She was unable to move. Unable to speak. All she could do was feel.

And then slowly, almost reluctantly, almost as though he expected her to refuse him, Brand bent his head and kissed her.

It was a light kiss. The feathering brush of his lips. The brief fan of his warm breath. It was over in the space of a blink. Yet there was a quality of tenderness about the caress that stayed with Cassie for hours.

Chapter Eleven

Exhaling on a restless sigh, Cassie plunked herself down on the edge of the bed in room 114 of the Bide-a-While Motel and stretched her legs out in front of her. She flexed her toes against the canvas of her sneakers and rubbed the back of her neck with one palm.

If she listened closely, she could hear Brand moving around in the adjoining room. As far as the cast and crew of *Prodigal* were concerned, he was using that room as an office. Production conferences were held in there. Dailies were screened in there, too. No one knew that Brand slept in there, as well.

No one except her and Brand.

Lies. Lies and more lies. They were eating away at her.

Cassie closed her eyes and prayed for strength.

She started at the sound of a fist rapping against the door that connected the two rooms. "Cassie?" Brand's voice inquired.

"Come in," she responded, opening her eyes and getting to her feet. She didn't need to unlock the connecting door.

She didn't bother to throw the bolt on it at night. She was painfully aware that there was no reason to do such a thing. Despite the kiss Brand had given her the day before, she'd reconciled herself to the fact that he didn't want her as a woman.

At least, she'd *tried* to reconcile herself to it.

Cassie still couldn't control the sudden speedup of her pulse each time she saw Brand. She couldn't prevent her breath from wedging in her throat each time she heard him speak her name, either. And she certainly couldn't stop herself from yearning for his kisses and caresses—even though she understood that they were as devoid of meaning for him as the rings he'd placed on her left hand.

What she *could* do was hide her true feelings and cling to the shredded vestiges of her pride. Pride was all Cassie had left. It was the only thing standing between her and utter disaster. Without pride to stop her, she knew she would have opened the connecting door between their rooms the first night they'd arrived and begged Brand to make love to her.

The connecting door swung open. Brand took a step or two into the room, then stopped, folding his arms across his chest. He was clad in running shoes, fraying khaki cutoffs and a T-shirt emblazoned with the words *Yes. It's Hot Enough for Me.*

Cassie saw him survey the rumpled bed she'd been sitting on. His lips thinned. Then his gaze shifted and settled on her. His lips thinned even more. Small whitened indentations appeared at the corners of his mouth.

"I sincerely hope that's not what you're planning to wear today," he said finally. His voice was tight.

Cassie blinked, taken aback. She glanced down at herself, wondering what possible objection Brand could have to the white duck shorts and white-and-turquoise tank top she had on. Crisp, cool and comfortable, the outfit was another of the purchases she'd made during her Rodeo Drive spending spree. She looked back at Brand, trying to figure out what was going on.

"Are you worried about me getting a sunburn?" she asked tentatively. That seemed to be the only rational explanation for his comment. "You don't have to. I've got a tube of zinc oxide for my nose and I plan to slather myself with sunscreen every hour on the hour."

Brand's nostrils flared on a sudden intake of breath and something dangerous sparked to life in the depths of his eyes. "If you weren't showing so much skin, you wouldn't have to plan on devoting so much time to slathering," he returned caustically. He pronounced the word "slathering" as though it were some kind of perversion.

Cassie's heart skipped a beat. "I beg your pardon?"

"You heard what I said."

"Yes, I heard what you said," she agreed with an edge. "I'm just not sure I believe you actually said it."

"Do you think I approve of you flaunting yourself the way you've been doing?"

"Flaunting myself!"

Brand's eyes ran over her, cataloging every line of her slender body. Cassie felt her nipples pucker against the fragile fabric of her bra. She knew the physical response must be evident beneath the thin cotton tank top.

"What would you call it?" he asked.

"Dressing sensibly!" Cassie retorted, managing to drag her voice back down to within a half octave of its normal pitch. She quelled an urge to cross her arms in front of her breasts. "It's supposed to be more than ninety degrees in the shade today, Brand." She glared at him, then demanded, "Just who do you think you are, telling me what I can and can't wear?"

"I'm your husband."

Somewhere in the back of her mind, Cassie realized that if she'd had something in her hands at that moment, she would have thrown it at Brand's arrogantly attractive face. "How *dare* you—"

Knock. Knock. Knock.

"Brand? Cassie?"

It could have been anyone knocking on the door. But the voice calling both their names was very definitely Lee Allen's.

Cassie started to tremble. Her stomach twisted.

Knock. Knock. Knock.

"Hello?"

Brand uttered a four-letter word he'd never used in Cassie's presence before. She flinched at the savagery with which he spit out the single syllable, but she was beyond being troubled by the word itself.

I'm your husband.

Your husband.

Cassie sank down on the edge of the unmade bed, clasping her hands together tightly. Her palms felt damp and clammy. The rings on her left hand dug into the flesh of her fingers. She didn't care about the pain. In an odd way, she welcomed it.

I'm your husband.

How could Brand even think that? He was no more her husband than she was his wife.

Knock. Knock. Knock.

"Anybody home?"

Brand gave Cassie a searing glance that promised their quarrel was far from over. Then he stalked across the room in four long strides, undid the dead bolt, yanked off the safety chain and jerked the door open with far more force than was necessary.

"Hi, Brand," she heard Lee say in a remarkably cheerful voice. "I have those papers you wanted to take a look at."

"Thanks, Lee," Brand replied coolly. "I'll be with you in a second." He shut the door and turned back toward Cassie. Although her stomach was still churning and she couldn't completely stop the shudders running through her, she met his gaze evenly. "Are you going to change?" he asked.

Deliberately, defiantly, Cassie shook her head.

* * *

Cassie was still fuming about the episode in the motel room six hours later as she stood beneath the blazing Texas sun and watched Brand rehearse a complex tracking shot that required the absolute coordination of the cast and crew. A part of her marveled at the single-minded intensity he brought to the task. Another part of her—a much greater part—mightily resented the fact that he appeared to be suffering no residual effects from their earlier argument.

The technical setup for this particular sequence had already been going on for ninety minutes. Graham Wyatt and Sheila Parker had long since retreated to the comfort of the air-conditioned trailer, which—like their rented home and housekeeper—had been one of the perks mandated by their contracts. Their disappearance had obviously disappointed the local folk who had gathered to watch the filming. Yet judging by some of the comments she'd overheard, Cassie suspected that more than a few of the people who had come to see Graham and Sheila had stayed to observe Brand in action.

"Damn him," she muttered under her breath, wiping her forearm across her forehead. Since the former was as damp with perspiration as the latter, the gesture didn't help much. She fanned herself with one hand and held the front of her tank top away from her body with the other. She felt a bead of sweat trickle down between her shoulder blades.

There was nothing—not one thing—wrong with the way she was dressed, Cassie told herself for the twentieth or thirtieth time. All right, so one strap of the top slid off her shoulder now and again. She could shove it back into place. And maybe the shorts were a couple of millimeters snugger than she might have liked, but that didn't mean the outfit was indecent!

Yet Brand had behaved as though she'd decided to prance around the set wearing a see-through lace top and a string bikini bottom. Flaunting herself, indeed! Even her uncle had never said anything quite that pompously judgmental. What did the man expect her to do? Dress in long-sleeved muumuus and orthopedic shoes like Eula Mae Bertram?

Just who do you think you are, telling me what I can and can't wear? she'd demanded of him.

I'm your husband, he'd replied.

Cassie clenched her hands and stared at Brand.

"Her husband" was dressed far less modestly than she at this point. His T-shirt had become sodden with sweat hours before and he'd pulled it off, mopped his chest with it, then carelessly tossed the garment aside.

He'd remained stripped to the waist since that time. The sleek, toned muscles of his shoulders, back and arms rippled subtly beneath his sun-bronzed skin each time he gestured. Several times he'd jammed his hands deep into the back pockets of his khaki shorts, pulling the cutoffs tight across the front. There had been nothing subtle about what this had revealed.

Suppressing a moan of distress, Cassie closed her eyes. She was aware of the tightening of her breasts, of the aching emptiness in the lower part of her body.

She was going to have to quit Marcus Moviemaking. That much was now painfully clear to her. Once *Prodigal* was finished and she and Brand put an end to their make-believe marriage, she was going to have to sever all her ties to the man she loved. To continue as his assistant would force her to continue lying . . . hiding . . . hurting. That was something she knew she couldn't endure.

"Cassie?"

The voice was Lee Allen's. So, Cassie assumed, were the pleasantly cool fingers touching her bare forearm. She opened her eyes, blinking against the merciless glare of the sun.

"Yes, Lee?"

"You look like you could use this," the location manager said, extending a can of soda. The aluminum container was beaded with condensation, indicating the liquid inside was cold.

Cassie stared at the can blankly for a moment, then ran her tongue over her upper lip, tasting salt. "Thank you," she said, accepting the unexpected offering. She popped the top and took a drink. The icy beverage bathed her throat like a blessing. After a moment, she lifted the can to her face, rubbing it against one cheek and then the other.

"Good?" Lee inquired with a knowing grin.

"Wonderful," Cassie agreed with a crooked smile, then took another greedy swallow of the chilled soda. The carbonation tickled the inside of her nose. Her gaze started to wander in Brand's direction. She forced herself to concentrate on the man beside her.

"Hot enough for you?" Lee inquired. His dark eyes flicked up and down her body.

Cassie grimaced, remembering the slogan on Brand's T-shirt. "Did you make that up all by yourself, Lee?"

He chuckled. "Nah. Must have read it somewhere." He relieved her of the soda he'd given her, took a gulp, then returned the can. He made a small burping sound and wiped his mouth with the back of his hand.

"You're welcome," Cassie told him wryly.

The location manager shrugged. He cocked his curly head to one side and studied her with disconcerting directness, saying nothing.

Cassie shifted uncomfortably. She knew she'd garnered more than a few unusually long looks from members of the production crew over the past few hours. Nothing offensive, just unsettling, given the argument she and Brand had had. And now to have Lee Allen checking her out...

She took another drink of soda, then asked, "What?"

"You're freckling like crazy, you know," the location manager answered. "And I think your back's starting to burn. You want me to slather some sunscreen on you?"

Cassie's eyes widened. While Lee was smiling blandly, she knew the word "slather" hadn't come out of his mouth by chance.

"You overheard us this morning," she said tightly, prickles of apprehension running up and down her spine.

"Yeah." The admission was unadorned and unabashed. "Through the window. Soundproofing doesn't seem to be a priority at the Bide-a-While. I won't go into what I heard going on in the room next to mine two nights ago."

Cassie frantically reviewed the quarrel she'd had with Brand. Had either of them said anything that might allow Lee to deduce the truth about their relationship? she wondered.

"Oh, don't look so worried, Cassie," the location manager advised. He borrowed the can of soda from her again and helped himself to another long swallow. "I'm not going to say anything to anybody. But I have to tell you—I understand why Brand was so hot and bothered this morning."

Cassie stiffened. "In other words, you think there's something wrong with the way I'm dressed, too."

Lee shook his head. "No. Not exactly."

"What does that mean?"

The location manager appeared to consider his answer to this question very carefully. "It means that if I were married to you, I'd probably insist you wear a pup tent," he declared. "A husband likes to have his wife admired, Cassie. But not too much. If you catch my drift."

Cassie supposed Lee's comments might make some sense if she and Brand had a real marriage. Unfortunately all she and Brand had was a sham, so what the location manager was saying didn't matter one whit.

"Well, do you or don't you want me to slather some sunscreen on you?" Lee asked after a few moments.

Cassie hesitated, suddenly becoming aware of a faintly unpleasant tingling in the skin of her back and shoulders. "All right," she said with a little nod. "Thank you." She bent to rummage through her faithful canvas tote bag. After a few seconds, she located the squeeze bottle of sunscreen she'd been using and started to straighten up. "If you'd just rub some of this on my..." Her voice trailed off as she got a look at the expression on Lee's face. In the same instant, every nerve in her body started clamoring out an alarm.

Brand, Cassie thought as a frisson of apprehension danced through her. She turned around very slowly, clutching the bottle of sunscreen like a talisman.

Brand was standing no more than two feet away from her. He was still half-naked, clad in nothing but the khaki shorts and running shoes. His torso was sheened with perspiration and streaked with dust. His hair was slicked back from his forehead and the strongly molded features of his face were set. He looked tired, but very tough.

"I think I should do that," he said quietly. His voice was cool. His eyes were not.

"Good point, Brand," Lee Allen agreed hastily. "See you later, Cassie."

Some elemental feminine instinct brought Cassie close to panic in the next few seconds. She stared up into Brand's compelling face, her pulse pounding and her mouth dry. "What about the setup?" she managed to get out.

"I called a break," Brand replied, stepping forward and taking the bottle of sunscreen from her nerveless fingers. "Apparently you didn't hear me. Turn around."

"You don't have to—"

"Turn around, Cassie."

Cassie did as she was told. She had the feeling Brand would enforce his order physically if she didn't. She stood with her back to him for several unnerving seconds, forcing herself not to tremble. She half expected to feel his fingers circle her throat and start to squeeze.

She gasped when Brand finally did touch her. He laid his hands flat against the bare skin of her upper back. His palms were slick with sunscreen. The feel of them pressing against her flesh triggered a fluttering deep in her stomach.

After a few moments, he began a slow, stroking massage. He traced the top of her spine with the faintly callused balls of his thumbs, releasing a quicksilver cascade of pleasure within her. Cassie caught her lower lip between her teeth, trying to resist the treacherous onslaught of sensation.

"Relax, dammit."

He might as well have commanded her to flap her arms and fly. "I can't."

"You looked perfectly at ease before."

"You weren't angry at me before."

"Would you care to bet on that?" His voice was low and harsh.

Cassie made a little sound of protest. "What...what have I done?"

"What haven't you done?" he countered, lifting his hands away from her. Cassie made a movement of withdrawal. "Stay still," he ordered. "I'm not finished with you yet."

Cassie heard the sound of sunscreen lotion being squirted out of the bottle. After a second, she felt Brand's hands settle back on her shoulders. His palms curved over her as though staking a claim. His fingertips brushed the edge of her collarbone. He began to slide his hands forward.

Cassie was bitterly aware that he was punishing her for refusing to change her clothes. She was also acutely conscious that he had chosen a cruelly effective way of chastising her. Why he felt the need to hurt her, she didn't know.

"I'm sorry," she said, hating the weakness she heard in her voice.

Brand's hands stilled for an instant. "Sorry for what?"

"Everything." His hands started inching down again, his fingertips moving closer...closer...to the upper swell of her breasts. Cassie felt herself go hot, then cold, then hot again. Her vision blurred for an instant. "Anything."

"Everything and anything," Brand repeated. It was impossible to get a fix on his tone. "Well, I'm sorry, too, sweetheart."

The endearment hurt far more than an insult. Brand hadn't used that particular word since the night when they'd slept in the same bed in Palm Springs. She knew he hadn't meant it then and he certainly didn't mean it now.

Cassie drew a shaky breath. What Brand was doing to her was wrong. No matter that his touch made her blood heat, her body hum and her brain haze with longing, it was wrong.

She brought her hands up and caught his wrists. His fingers tightened against her flesh for a moment, then went slack. She turned her head, trying to look at him. What she could see of his expression told her almost nothing.

"Brand, please," she pleaded softly. "Stop."

"Why?"

"Because... because I can't stand much more of this."

She heard Brand inhale swiftly, then exhale very, very slowly.

"Neither can I" were the only words he said to her before he released her.

Afterward the only words he addressed to her were orders.

That night and the night that followed, Cassie locked the connecting door between their motel rooms.

Chapter Twelve

Happy birthday, dear Cassie," chorused the enthusiastic crowd of the *Prodigal* cast and crew members gathered on the deck of the Bide-a-While Motel swimming pool. "Happy birthday...to-o-o-o-o-o you-u-u-u-u-u!" An ill-advised attempt to sing the last two words in harmony dissolved into laughter and applause.

Cassie joined in the laughter. She glanced down at the garishly frosted sheet cake in front of her, then lifted her gaze to look at the people around her. She experienced a warm surge of affection for each and every one of them.

On the heels of that emotion came a rush of sadness. How many of these people would she ever get a chance to work with again? she wondered. Probably not very many, once *Prodigal* wrapped and she went through with her decision to quit Marcus Moviemaking.

Cassie felt the hot pinprick of tears forming in the corners of her eyes. She blinked and swallowed hard, then turned her head. She didn't want to, but she couldn't help herself. Brand was standing about five feet to her left and he drew her eyes the way a flame draws a moth. He had his arms folded across his chest and he was studying her intently. Unlike everyone else present, he was not smiling.

"Hey, hey, don't go all moony on me, Cassie," T. D. Tedeschi, Marcus Moviemaking's chief publicist, scolded. The proud possessor of a state-of-the-art camcorder, he was taping this event for posterity—and, he'd jokingly told Cassie earlier, for purposes of blackmail.

Cassie managed to gear her gaze away from Brand. She looked at the publicist questioningly. "What?"

"Can you and Brand cut the eyeball action for a few seconds?" T.D. requested grumpily. "This is supposed to be a happy scene, not a hot one. Think Disney. Now I want you to take a beat, then bend over and blow out the candles—okay?"

"Jeez, T.D.," one of the gaffers complained. "What do you think you are? A director?"

"What's Cassie's motivation for blowing out the candles?" someone else asked mockingly after the chortles and catcalls provoked by the previous quip had faded.

"Her motivation is that they're going to melt all over the cake if she doesn't," Brand interjected wryly.

Cassie glanced to her left once again.

"Cassie!" T.D. expostulated. "Come on!"

Flushing, Cassie forced her attention back to the task at hand. Holding her long, loose hair back from her face, she bent forward over the cake. She inhaled deeply and blew the candles out with one gusting breath. She straightened abruptly, feeling a bit light-headed.

"Speech, speech!" someone demanded.

"Yeah," someone else concurred. "Speech!"

The call was quickly taken up by the gathered throng. Cassie eventually gestured for quiet. "I don't know what to say," she admitted with a self-conscious little laugh once the clamor had died down.

"Give us your Oscar acceptance speech," Graham Wyatt suggested. He was standing off to the right, drinking from a long-necked bottle of beer. Sheila was next to him, looking very beautiful. She was clad in a clingy violet halter dress with a hammered silver belt. The sleekly feminine outfit was a far cry from the unflattering waitress uniform she'd worn earlier in the day for her role as Sally Harper. It also made Cassie wish she'd chosen to celebrate her twenty-fourth birthday in something a little more sophisticated than a two-piece white cotton dress and canvas espadrilles.

"My what?" Cassie asked, taken aback.

"Your Oscar acceptance speech."

"But I don't have..." Cassie's voice trailed off as she realized that she *did* have the outlines of an Oscar acceptance speech tucked away in the back of her brain. After all, she'd been fantasizing about winning Hollywood's most coveted prize since she was a teenager. Naturally that fantasizing had included mental rehearsals of the modest but memorable remarks she would one day deliver to the members of the National Academy of Motion Picture Arts and Sciences.

"Of course you have one," Graham returned with a knowing chuckle. "Everybody in the business does." There was a ripple of laughter at this assertion.

"Okay, okay," Cassie acquiesced with a smile. She paused for a moment, ordering her thoughts, then began. "What I want to say is this. Number one, I hope a *lot* of people get to deliver Oscar speeches because of *Prodigal*. Number two, I want to thank everyone for this party. And number three—let's have some cake!"

It was difficult to tell which of her three points the crowd approved of most. Each one was punctuated by cheers and clapping.

Cassie spent the next fifteen minutes serving cake and accepting cards and presents. Most of the gifts were gag items. More than a few were in questionable taste. Cassie blushed hotly several times, but felt absurdly pleased and touched. She understood that the tacky birthday tributes meant she was considered "one of the gang"—despite her marriage to Brand.

There were a few serious presents, of course. From Sheila Parker, who seemed to be in an odd and distracted mood, there was a bottle of her favorite perfume. Cassie wondered how the other woman had discovered her fragrance preference, but she didn't ask.

From Graham Wyatt there was an elegant inlaid picture frame with a photo of himself looking hot and unhappy in a suit of armor. Cassie instantly recognized the photo as a publicity still from *Saracen Steel*, the costume epic they'd spoken about a few days before.

"I hope you don't mind the picture of me," the actor said with a self-deprecating smile after kissing her lightly on the cheek. "It probably seems like the height of egomania."

"Not quite," Cassie teased. "You didn't autograph it."

"What?" Graham feigned shock and dismay. "Good heavens! Get me a pen!"

The last person to give Cassie a gift was Brand. He waited until the crowd of well-wishers had dispersed around the deck before coming over to her. She sensed his approach and turned to face him, her heart beating much more quickly than normal.

"Happy birthday," Brand said quietly.

"Thank you." So good so far, Cassie thought, shifting her weight from one foot to the other. She moistened her lips. "Would you, ah, like some cake?"

Brand shook his head, then held out a small box wrapped in silver paper. "This is for you."

She looked at the gift he was offering for a few seconds, but made no move to take it. "You didn't have to," she told him, raising her eyes to meet his.

"Yes, I did."

His answer stung. Cassie glanced away for a moment. She understood what he was saying, of course. Brand felt he "had" to give her a birthday present to maintain the facade of their supposedly loving relationship. She had no doubt that his gift would be expensive and exquisite. She also had no doubt that it had been selected with a great deal of calculation—but absolutely no caring.

"Please, Cassie. Take it."

Cassie looked back at Brand, then down at the gift. After a moment, she did as he'd asked. Willing herself to keep her fingers steady, she peeled back the foil paper, then opened the box.

What she saw was so far from what she'd expected to see that it took her a few seconds to accept the fact that she wasn't dreaming.

Inside the box was a shiny gold whistle engraved with her nickname. The *i* in "Cassie" was dotted with a tiny cabochon emerald. It was an expensive and exquisite item, to be sure; it was also imbued with a wonderful sense of whimsy.

Cassie started to laugh. The sound bubbled up out of her like water from an underground spring. It was fresh and unforced. She couldn't remember the last time she'd laughed so freely. Nor could she remember the last time she'd lifted her eyes to Brand and smiled at him as she did now.

She wanted to thank him—to share her heartfelt delight in his gift. But when Brand answered her smile with a very male one of his own, something happened to her ability to speak and breathe. A glorious kind of suffocation seized her. Her pulse rate rocketed. She felt the frantic force of it pounding in her throat and temples.

"I know you know how to whistle without one," Brand said in a voice that was deeper than usual. The sound of it affected Cassie like the stroke of a velvet glove. "But just in case..."

He lifted his right hand as he let this sentence trail off ambiguously. Gently, very gently, he cupped the left side of her face in his palm. His fingers curved carefully along the line of her neck, the ball of his thumb caressed the softness of her cheek.

"Just in c-case?" Cassie prompted in a shaky whisper.

"Say cheese," a vaguely familiar female voice commanded.

The voice belonged to Eula Mae Bertram.

So did the flash camera that went off in Cassie's face a split second later.

Just in case . . . what?

The question gnawed at Cassie on and off for the next three hours.

Brand hadn't answered her the first time she'd asked it. He would have, if Eula Mae Bertram hadn't intervened. Of that, Cassie was certain.

Exactly how he would have replied, she didn't know. She didn't know, but she could hope and she could dream. The unexpected present of the gold whistle had given her back the ability to do both.

Just in case—*what?*

Cassie had wanted to put the question to Brand a second time, but she hadn't had the chance. No sooner had Eula Mae Bertram waddled away than makeup artists Freddie and Francis had approached and demanded Cassie settle an argument they were having about one of her mother's movies. Simultaneously assistant director Tim Potter had materialized at Brand's elbow to talk about the coming week's shooting schedule.

Freddie and Francis had been supplanted by a burly electrician named Pete, who'd asked her to dance. A glance to her right had told her that Brand was engrossed in his discussion with Tim, so she'd accepted the invitation. After ably demonstrating that disco was not quite dead, Pete had reluctantly passed her on to another partner, a camera operator named Jake. Jake had eventually surrendered her to an extra named Bobby Ray Delbert, who had no sense of rhythm but lots of energy.

Cassie tried, several times, to return to Brand and reclaim his attention. She needed to know what he'd intended to say to her. She needed to know exactly what the gold whistle meant. Unfortunately what she needed and what the social dynamics of the party would allow her to have were two very different things.

Still, even though they ended up on opposite sides of the swimming pool, she managed to keep track of where Brand was and whom he was with. She had the oddest feeling he was keeping a similar watch on her.

It was nearing eleven when Cassie realized that she hadn't caught a glimpse of Brand in more than fifteen minutes. The realization made her uneasy and, after shaking her head to several invitations to dance, she began threading her way around the pool deck to the area where she'd last seen him.

She didn't find Brand, but she did run into Lee Allen.

Or to be more accurate, *Lee* ran into *her*. Cassie spotted the location manager standing by himself and came up behind him. She was just about to reach out and tap him on the shoulder when he took a sudden step backward and collided with her. As he turned around to apologize, he was jostled by someone else. The plastic cup he'd been holding went flying out of his hand and the dregs of the drink it had contained spilled down the front of Cassie's scoop-necked dress.

"Cassie!" Lee exclaimed, staring at the damage he'd caused with great dismay. "Oh, damn. Cassie, I'm sorry."

Cassie glanced down at the spreading liquor stain and grimaced. "It's all right, Lee," she said automatically.

"I didn't—I mean, somebody bumped my arm—"

"I know you didn't do it on purpose."

"Well, let me get you something to clean it up with." He gestured as though he expected the necessary items to materialize out of thin air.

"Don't bother." Cassie held the damp fabric of her bodice away from her skin. "It'll be easier for me to run back to the room and change."

Lee rolled his eyes. "I feel awful."

"It's no big deal." The volume of the music throbbing out of the multispeaker sound system that had been jury-rigged around the pool suddenly increased. Cassie leaned in and raised her voice to compete with the din. "Have you seen Brand?"

"What?"

"Brand! Have you seen Brand?"

The location manager looked blank for a second or so, then shook his head. "To tell the truth, I haven't seen much of anything for the past few minutes but bright white spots dancing before my eyes."

It took Cassie a moment to make sense out of this answer. "Eula Mae Bertram took your picture?"

Lee nodded. "It wasn't enough she made me fork over a thousand-dollar security deposit on the pool. Oh, no. I had to agree to let her play roving photographer, too. Did she do the 'say cheese' routine with you?"

"Unfortunately, yes," Cassie affirmed, suppressing a sigh. The question she wanted answered echoed through her head. She glanced around, searching for some sign of Brand. He's not here, she thought with sudden and unnerving certainty.

She looked back at her colleague. "Do you have *any* idea where Brand is, Lee?" she asked, slipping her free hand into the pocket of her softly gathered skirt. Her fingers closed around the gold whistle.

Lee shook his head. "No. Sorry, Cassie. The last time I saw him, he was watching you do the Texas two-step with one of the extras."

Cassie was halfway across the gravel parking lot of the Bide-a-While Motel when she realized that the light in her room was on. It was on, yet she distinctly remembered switching it off before she'd left for the party.

Brand, she thought, picking up her pace.

A few seconds later, she saw the silhouette of a man on the window shade.

Brand, she thought again, and walked even faster.

A few seconds after that, a second silhouette appeared on the window shade. This one was distinctly, devastatingly female.

Cassie halted. With eyes wide and heart hammering, she watched the man extend his hand. She watched the woman take it. She saw the way their fingers caught and clung. It was clear that the connection between the couple was more than physical.

Cassie wanted to turn and run. To pretend she hadn't seen. But she knew she couldn't. She began moving forward once again. Slowly. Carefully. She felt as though she were walking on a tightrope. One tiny misstep and she would come crashing down . . . down . . . down.

Cassie came to a stop just outside the window of her room. Reaching into her skirt pocket, she brought out Brand's birthday gift. She had no idea what she intended to do with it.

As Lee Allen had observed several days before, soundproofing was not a priority at the Bide-a-While. Although Cassie couldn't hear everything that was being said by the silhouetted figures, she could hear enough.

More than enough.

"What am I going to do, Brand?"

"You've got to tell him, Sheila."

"But, if I do—"

"—going to guess if you don't."

Cassie closed her eyes.

"Graham's so involved in the film maybe he won't—"

"—have to, Sheila."

"Oh, Brand. Everytime I think of it—"

"Shh, I know . . . I know."

Cassie opened her eyes.

Brand and Sheila were embracing.

Cassie let the gold whistle slip from her fingers and drop to the ground. Then she turned and ran.

* * *

Cassie tossed her head and glared at Lee Allen. "You think I'm drunk, don't you?" she asked accusingly. "Don't you?"

"I don't know what you are," the location manager returned grimly, trying to grab hold of her forearm. "But whatever it is, I don't like it."

In point of fact, Cassie was not drunk. A part of her would have liked to be. Given her current state of mind, the idea of using alcohol to obliterate the memory of what she'd seen and heard fifteen minutes before seemed very seductive. She'd actually tried to choke down a shot of tequila when she'd initially returned to the party. The taste of the potent liquor had sickened her, however, and she'd abandoned the glass after the first sip.

Exactly why she'd come back to the party at all, Cassie didn't know for sure. Deep down, she suspected it was because she was afraid to be alone with the images in her head.

Brand and Sheila.

Sheila and Brand.

In each other arms. *Together.*

He'd lied to her. She loved him and he'd lied to her. He'd lied to her over and over and over again.

Cassie jerked away from Lee. "I'm soberer than you are!" she told him angrily.

"Well, that's hardly going to win you a good-conduct medal. Cassie—honey, please! Just come away from the edge of the pool and sit down for a few minutes, okay? I'll go find Brand—"

"No!" The last thing she wanted was for anyone—anyone!—to find Brand.

"But, sweetheart—"

"Don't call me that!"

"All right, all right," Lee agreed quickly, throwing up his hands in a gesture of surrender. "I won't call you that." He glanced around, clearly getting a bit desperate. The party was becoming rowdier by the minute. "Ah, what do you say we go for a walk? I'll take you back to your room and you can change your clothes."

Cassie shook her head violently. The thought of going anywhere near her room made her physically ill.

"C'mon," Lee coaxed. "We can look for Brand—"

"Hey, Cassie! I been searchin' all over for you."

The drawling male voice belonged to the extra she'd danced with earlier. Cassie whirled away from Lee, away from his references to Brand. "Bobby!" she exclaimed.

The Texan waggled his fingers at her. His posture was about ten degrees off plumb to the right. The broad grin he had plastered across his face was about ten degrees off plumb to the left. "You wanna dance with me again, Cassie?" he inquired.

Lee caught Cassie's right arm and tried to pull her back around to face him. "Butt out, Texas," he snarled.

Bobby blinked and took a step forward. "My name is Bobby Ray Delbert."

"I don't care if your name is the Lone Ranger! Stay out of this."

"Let go of me!" Cassie demanded, twisting in Lee's grasp.

"Dammit, Cassie! Will you stop fighting me?"

Bobby blinked again and took another step forward. He latched on to Cassie's left arm. "I'll thank you not to use that kind of language when a lady's present," he said ominously. He pulled Cassie toward him.

"Listen, Delbert," Lee countered, tugging Cassie in the opposite direction. "This *lady* is a married woman and her husband is going to show up any second!"

Trapped like a wishbone between the angry location manager and the inebriated extra, Cassie felt something inside her snap. "I don't have a husband!" she declared shrilly, struggling against both men.

"Yes, you do," an unmistakable male voice contradicted.

Lee and Bobby released Cassie in the same split second. Completely off balance, she staggered back a step, arms windmilling in a futile effort to keep herself standing upright. The sole of her espadrille skidded on something and her foot slid out from under her.

"Brand!" she cried and toppled into the pool with a tremendous splash.

Chapter Thirteen

Cassie's memories of the next ten minutes were never very clear. The only details she could ever recall involved Brand . . . and only Brand.

Brand was the one who'd hauled her out of the swimming pool. His handling of her had been rough and he'd been cursing with quiet fury all the while. She'd caught a single glimpse of his face through the tangle of her soaking wet hair. He'd been white beneath his tan and his blue eyes had been blazing.

Brand was the one who'd pounded her on the back as she'd coughed up several ounces of highly chlorinated water. Again his treatment of her had been less than gentle and he'd still been swearing with soft, barely suppressed violence.

Brand was the one who'd helped her struggle to her feet, too. He was the one who'd steadied her when she'd swayed uncertainly, then scooped her up into his arms when she'd swayed a second time. He'd held her hard against him, shaking his head to all offers of assistance. She'd gotten a second glimpse of his face then. He'd regained a little color, but his sky-colored eyes had still been searingly bright.

And finally, Brand was the one who'd carried her across the motel parking lot and into the room they ostensibly had been living in as husband and wife. Cassie had turned her face into his neck during the brief journey, still too dazed to really register what was happening. She'd lost herself in the smooth rhythm of his rapid stride. Her mouth had brushed the side of his throat for an instant, and she'd felt the sudden jump of his pulse against her lips.

Somewhere between the moment Brand deposited her on the end of their supposedly conjugal bed and the moment he stalked across to the door and threw the bolt, Cassie's shock-hazed brain started to function again. She realized exactly where she was. She remembered exactly what had gone on there less than an hour before.

"No!" she cried, levering herself into a sitting position. Kicking off her squishy-wet canvas espadrilles, she lurched to her feet. She could feel small rivulets of water dribbling down the length of her body. Her clothes clung to her breasts and thighs like transparent adhesive tape.

Brand turned. There was a dark and dangerous flush on his cheekbones. His eyes, which had been as bright as blowtorches only a few minutes before, had become as bleakly frigid as arctic tundra. "No, what?"

Cassie didn't care how cold Brand's eyes were. The anger burning inside her could survive another ice age. "Just no," she spat, pushing drippy strands of hair off her face. "I want you to get out."

Brand shook his head. His features were set, every line of his lean body was stiff. "Not yet."

"Yes!"

Another head shake. "Not until you tell me what the hell is wrong with you."

Given all that had happened, Cassie had thought she was beyond being shocked by anything Brand said or did. In the space of one short sentence she discovered that she'd either overestimated herself or underestimated him.

"M-m-me?" she sputtered. "You want to know what's wrong with *me*? Why don't you figure out what's wrong with *you*!"

"I don't have to figure it out. I already know. You're what's wrong with me."

Cassie felt the blood drain out of her face.

"Every second . . . of every minute . . . of every hour . . . of every day," Brand went on. His voice was raw. "It's hell being with you. It's hell being without you."

Now it was her turn to shake her head. "No."

Brand started to walk forward. Cassie began backing up.

"Yes," he insisted. "I know—"

"You know nothing!"

"I know how you make me feel, Cassie."

Like hell. He'd said she made him feel like hell. "You're crazy!"

His mouth twisted. "Very probably."

"What about Sheila?" Cassie flung the actress's name at him like a stone, hoping to hurt him, hoping to halt his inexorable progress toward her. She spared a quick glance over her shoulder. The wall was only a few steps away.

Brand seemed to check himself for a split second. Then he resumed his advance. "This isn't about Sheila," he replied.

"Oh, yes, it is," Cassie countered tautly, still edging backward. Dear heaven, she'd *seen* them together. She'd *heard* them together. She knew! She knew everything. She knew she'd been deceived almost as cruelly as Graham Wyatt had been.

"No, it isn't. This is about you and me."

In that moment, Cassie came very close to hating Brand. "There is no you and me," she said shakily. "There never has been. All there's been is lies on top of lies on top of more lies."

At that point, she ran out of maneuvering room. An instant later, Brand closed most of the distance between them. He stopped directly in front of her, leaving only inches separating their bodies. He placed his hands on either side of her head, palms pressed flat against the wall.

"Then let's stop lying," he said quietly. "Let's tell the truth."

Cassie closed her eyes.

The truth. She didn't think she knew what the truth was anymore.

"Cassie?"

She opened her eyes and looked up into Brand's compelling face. She felt the heat of his body through her wet clothes, felt the fan of his breath against her damp cheek.

"The truth is," she said in a voice as brittle as spun glass, "I want you to leave me alone."

He didn't move. His expression didn't change. Only the sudden dilation of his pupils told Cassie that he'd heard her words. Whether those words had been true or false, she couldn't say.

After several long, silent seconds, Brand drew an unsteady breath. "The truth is," he responded, "I don't think I can."

Cassie started to tremble. "You're a liar."

He flinched. When he spoke, his voice was very low and very gentle. "Not about that."

"About everything."

"Not about that, Cassie," he repeated. His eyes darkened the way the sky did at dusk. "And not about this."

"This" began with him capturing her face between his hands. His hard palms curved to fit the line of her cheeks, his lean fingers splayed to delve deep into the tangle of her wet hair. His hold on her tightened after a few seconds and he tilted her head back.

"Oh, Cassie," he whispered thickly. Cassie felt a tremor run through him. Slowly he dipped his head to claim her mouth.

There was an instant of brushing contact, then their lips caught and clung. Brand's breath joined with hers. Cassie heard someone whimper and realized it must be her.

There was nothing calculated or controlled, nothing practiced or precise, about the kiss Brand gave her. Cassie might have been able to resist if there had been. Instead his kiss was deep, devouring and a little bit desperate. Her only instinct was to respond.

"Cassie...oh, sweet..." Brand groaned against her mouth. The rough velvet sound of his voice sent white-hot shivers dancing along her nervous system. He raked the edge of one tooth lightly against her lower lip, then licked the same spot. Cassie felt her bones begin to liquify.

She brought her arms up and circled his neck, linking her fingers together behind his head. She arched into the embrace, wanting to get closer to him. Brand shifted his body, answering her unspoken desire. She parted her lips to say his name. Her intention was swept aside by the greedy, gliding intrusion of his tongue.

Cassie shuddered as Brand's hands stroked downward over her body. From shoulders to breasts—cupping, caressing. From breasts to hips—molding, massaging.

A single button held the waistband of her skirt closed. Brand sought it, found it and undid it. Cassie felt the sodden garment slide down her legs and puddle around her ankles. A moment later, Brand bent and slipped an arm behind her knees. He lifted her off her feet and carried her back to the bed they had never shared.

Endless, erotic minutes elapsed before they were both totally naked. The need to kiss and caress delayed completion of the task even more than the sudden and uncharacteristic clumsiness of Brand's fingers. Prompted by a fevered need to feel flesh against flesh, skin against skin, Cassie tried to help him with the undressing, but she repeatedly lost track of what she was doing. Discoveries about the nature of pleasure—and pleasuring—kept distracting her.

Finally Brand eased her back against the mattress, then stretched out beside her. He studied her with heavy-lidded eyes, his gaze full of midnight fire. Everywhere he looked, she burned. She felt no anxiety, no uncertainty. Only eagerness and anticipation. She stared at him wonderingly, then reached out as though to assure herself that he—and what was happening to her—were real.

Brand caught her hand and pressed it against his chest. She felt the beat of his heart through her fingertips.

"Brand," she whispered. "Oh, Brand. Yes . . . yes."

He saw the beauty no other man had ever seen.

He touched the secret softness no other man had ever touched.

He heard the yearning, broken cries no man had ever wrung from her lips.

And in the end, he received the gift only one man could ever be given.

For Cassie, the moment of surrender and the shattering rush of ecstasy that followed seemed both inevitable . . . and overwhelming.

Cassie surfaced out of a deep sleep late the next morning. Her return to consciousness did not happen instantly. The process was a languid one, punctuated by soft murmurs and slow movements.

She was dreamily aware of the fact that she was naked. The bed sheets rubbed and rustled pleasantly against her skin each time she shifted her body. She was also conscious of an unfamiliar feeling of fullness in her breasts and a faint throb of tenderness between her thighs.

She remembered what had happened. There was no shocking rush of memories. Rather recollection seeped in gradually, suffusing her with a delicious sense of satisfaction.

Wonderful. It had been wonderful. Nothing she had ever heard or read or seen—nothing she'd ever imagined—had prepared her for what she had experienced the night before.

Cassie had one long and lovely moment of total happiness. One long and lovely moment when she told herself that everything was going to be all right.

Yes. Yes. No more lies. Just the truth.

She and Brand.

Brand and . . . Sheila.

Cassie's moment of happiness came to an end. She opened her eyes and stared at the plaster ceiling overhead. Clutching the sheet to her breasts like a shield, she sat up.

She was alone in the bed, but not in the room. Brand was there, too. He was fully dressed and he was packing one of her suitcases with swift and silent efficiency. A sudden spasm of emotion racked her as she watched him handling her most personal belongings.

Perhaps Brand heard the creak of the mattress springs when she sat up. Perhaps she made some kind of sound and he was alerted by that. Then again, perhaps he simply sensed her awakening as he seemed to sense so many other things. Whatever the case, Cassie saw Brand suddenly stop what he was doing. His hands—the hands that had wooed her and won her the night before—went still. He lifted his dark head and looked at her.

What he saw when he looked, Cassie had no idea. His face was closed and shuttered, his vivid eyes devoid of all emotion but a steely kind of determination.

Cassie tried to say his name but her throat closed up and the word got stuck at the top of it. She swallowed convulsively, a shudder of apprehension running through her. "What?" she finally forced out.

"I had a call about an hour ago."

"A call?" Cassie hooked her hair back behind her ears with trembling fingers. She had a dim recollection of the shrill of the telephone in the other room rousing her about an hour before. She had a more vivid memory of Brand soothing her back to sleep with an intimate caress and a whispered assurance that he would take care of everything.

He'd gotten out of bed and he'd never come back.

"Your uncle was in a car accident last night."

Cassie gasped, her mind flooding with horrible images. For an instant she was a child again and trying to comprehend the nature of the terrible thing that had happened to her parents. An icy knot of fear formed in the pit of her stomach.

Something seemed to crack beneath the surface of Brand's carefully controlled expression. He took a step away from the suitcase and toward the bed. "Jordan's going to be fine, Cassie," he said quickly, convincingly. "He's got a case of whiplash and he's mad as hell because the back of his brand new Jag XJ-S is bashed in, but he's basically all right."

"Are you . . . are you sure?"

"Yes, positive. I spoke to him myself."

The icy knot of fear that had formed in the pit of Cassie's stomach melted just a little. Her eyes darted toward the connecting door, then back to Brand's face. "He was the one who called?"

Brand nodded.

"Didn't he ask to talk to me?"

"I told him you were asleep and I didn't want to wake you." Cassie saw his throat work. "I also told him you'd speak to him when you got back to L.A. this evening."

Cassie blinked several times. "L.A.?" she echoed in a bewildered tone. "Why should I go back to L.A.?"

"To see Jordan."

The icy knot in Cassie's stomach froze up solid once again. "You said he was all right!"

"He is. But your wanting to see him after his accident is the best explanation we can offer for your leaving."

There was an awful pause. Cassie stared at Brand, trying to make sense of what he was saying and why he was saying it. She wasn't so naïve as to truly believe that what had happened between them the night before was going to resolve all their problems. But she had hoped it would be a starting point. She knew they had shared something very, very special. Surely they could build on that sharing?

"I don't understand, Brand," she admitted finally.

Brand turned away. "You can't stay here, Cassie. Not now."

"But why—"

His gaze slammed back into hers. "Because I can't promise you that what happened last night won't happen again," he informed her harshly, then pressed his lips together as though he was afraid of saying too much.

"I never expected you to promise that," she said slowly. "What happened last night—"

"What happened last night was a mistake."

"No!" Her denial of his description was instant and from the heart. "What happened last was wonderful!"

Brand shook his head. "You don't know what you're saying."

"Yes, I do!" she insisted, gesturing with both hands. "I love you!"

"Don't!" His voice clashed with hers and prevailed through sheer force of will. "Cassie, please. Please, don't."

"But—"

"You don't love me," he said fiercely, finally approaching the bed. His hands were clenched at his sides. "You may believe you do right now, but you don't."

She looked up at him. "You think you understand my feelings better than I do?"

"Yes."

"How can you? I am not a child!"

Brand's gaze flicked downward. Cassie glanced down, too, and saw that the sheet she'd been holding against her had slipped out of position, nearly baring her breasts. Flushing, she pulled it back up into place.

Brand's eyes sought, found and held hers once again. "I know you're not a child," he told her quietly. "But I also know that, until last night, until . . . me, you were a virgin."

Cassie tightened her grip on the bedsheets and dipped her head a little. Her hair swung forward to veil the sides of her face. She said nothing. She didn't know what she could say. She hadn't realized her innocence had been so obvious. She wondered painfully just how awkward and inexperienced she had seemed to Brand.

"Why didn't you tell me, Cassie?" he asked.

She thought she heard accusation in his tone and she raised her head abruptly. "I tried to."

"When?"

"That night at the restaurant with Chet Walker. I tried to tell you that what you thought about us—about me and him—was wrong. But you said you didn't want to hear. Not then, not ever."

Brand's mouth thinned. The tanned skin of his face was pulled taut against his cheekbones.

"Does it make such a difference?" Cassie cried.

"It makes all the difference in the world. I never would have done what I did to you—"

"What *you* did to *me*?" she echoed, shocked to the core of his perception of what had happened. "We made love, Brand! We made love—together!"

"We made a mistake. A mistake we can't completely undo, I know. But it's a mistake I'm not going to let happen again."

"And so you're sending me away." Cassie realized that what Brand intended for her was no temporary exile. When she left, it would be over. She felt as though she was breaking apart inside. She wanted to weep, but the pain was too great.

"Yes."

She lifted her chin. "What if I won't go?"

An emotion flickered deep in his eyes. Cassie thought it looked like pity. The idea that Brand felt sorry for her was a sickening one.

"I'm not giving you a choice," he said very quietly.

They were at the bottom line and Cassie knew it. Brand didn't have to spell out what he meant. He'd made his decision, he had the authority to enforce it. There would be no appeal.

She sensed he was waiting for her to say something. But what could she say? The one thing that mattered—that she loved him—he obviously didn't want to hear. She sustained his gaze for as long as she could, then looked away.

Some silences seem to fill a room. Cassie felt the one that formed now was capable of emptying the universe. Still, as aching and awful as the silence was, she didn't speak.

Brand finally did. He said her name with great reluctance.

"What?" she asked after several moments, keeping her eyes averted.

"There may be consequences because of last night, you realize."

Her gaze swung back to collide with his. "Consequences?"

"I may have made you pregnant."

Cassie felt her eyes go wide and her face turn white. This was something she hadn't even considered. She did a quick calculation. She knew the conclusion she drew should have relieved her. Instead she felt a terrible pang of regret.

"I don't think you have to worry about that," she told him flatly.

"If you are, I want to know."

Cassie had a sudden, savage need to lash out at him. "Why?" she demanded. "So you can take responsibility for your mistake?"

She saw the barb hit home. She felt a split second of satisfaction. Then she remembered the circumstances of Brand's birth and childhood. He'd grown up knowing that neither the man who'd fathered him nor the woman who'd bore him had wanted him. He'd been a "mistake," and he'd been abandoned because of it.

She opened her mouth to say she was sorry, but he forestalled her apology.

"If that's the way you want to put it, yes," he responded grimly. He paused a beat, then went on. "If you're not pregnant, you can start divorce proceedings against me. I'm sure your uncle will give you the name of a good lawyer."

"What do I tell him?" Cassie didn't know whether she was referring to her uncle or the lawyer. It didn't really seem to matter.

Brand smiled so bleakly it broke her heart. "Tell him the truth. Tell him I'm a bastard and you never should have married me."

Chapter Fourteen

Nine days later, Cassandra Leigh Addams Marcus pulled into her husband's reserved parking spot in front of the Marcus Moviemaking offices. She'd been using Brand's space since she'd returned to work the previous Monday. She was certain people must have noticed, but no one had said anything about it to her.

Then again, no one had said much of anything about anything to her since her return from Texas. On the surface, her colleagues had appeared to accept her explanation that she had come back to L.A. out of concern for her uncle. No one had mentioned the fact that this concern might be wasted on a man who, according to industry gossip, had closed a multimillion-dollar deal for a client while awaiting an examination by an emergency room doctor.

Cassie shut off her car's engine and closed her eyes, thinking about her uncle. She knew *he* knew there was something terribly wrong. She suspected he'd known it before she'd arrived back in Los Angeles. Yet like her co-workers, he'd pretended there was nothing odd about her precipitous return or her protracted stay.

Until the night before.

He'd taken her out to dinner at a quiet restaurant that had never been mentioned in any gossip column she'd ever read. The place had been devoid of celebrities and there hadn't been a single cellular phone in sight. Cassie hadn't doubted for an instant why he'd selected it, and she'd braced herself to endure an evening of questions and conjecture.

Her uncle had waited until dessert before broaching the subject she'd known was foremost in both their minds.

"I know something's wrong between you and Brand, Cassie," he'd said without preamble. "I don't know what it is, but I feel responsible."

She'd been toying listlessly with a serving of half-melted mango sorbet. After a moment, she'd set down her spoon and gazed across the table at him. "Don't, Uncle Jordan," she'd responded quietly.

"If I hadn't forced the two of you—"

"You didn't force us."

He'd cocked his head, eyes very intent. "You're saying you and Brand would have gotten married without my interference?"

"I'm saying you shouldn't feel responsible."

Her uncle had shifted his weight and leaned in slightly, his movement more awkward than usual because of the padded neck brace he wore. The brace was the only visible reminder of his accident. "Did you want to marry him?" he asked bluntly.

Cassie's throat had tightened. She'd wanted to lie or look away, but she hadn't. Something inside her said she'd been doing too much of both during the past week and a half.

"Yes," she'd answered, rubbing the ball of her left thumb against the two rings she still wore on her left hand. "I wanted to marry Brand."

"And now?"

"And now—what?"

"You're married. But you're here and he's in Texas. What do you want now?"

She'd almost told him. She'd almost told him of the impossible dream she still cherished in her heart. But pride had made her say, "What I want is to stop talking about this."

"Cassie—"

"No," she interrupted, shaking her head. "Uncle Jordan, please. There's nothing you can do. I wouldn't want you to even if you could. Brand and I—it's *our* marriage. Ours. And no matter how it came to pass or how it ends up, it's between the two of us. Nobody else."

She'd shivered a little then, the echoes of a conversation reverberating through her mind.

This isn't about Sheila.

Oh, yes it is.

No, it isn't. It's about you and me.

There is no you and me. There never has been...

She glimpsed an odd expression in her uncle's gray eyes at that point and wondered what he must be reading in her face. "I see," he'd answered slowly.

"Do you?"

"Yes," he'd affirmed, nodding his head just a little. "I do."

And then, astonishingly, he'd let the subject drop.

At first Cassie hadn't understood why he'd done so. She'd expected him to keep pressing for answers, to start offering advice or vowing to take action of his own. That was how the Uncle Jordan she knew and loved had always behaved toward her in the past.

Comprehension had come suddenly, jolting her to the core. She'd realized that her uncle had acquiesced to her wishes rather than bulldozing over them "for their own good" because he'd finally stopping thinking of her as a child. Something had made him accept her as an adult.

Cassie blinked, coming back to the present with a start.

"I am not a child," she whispered aloud. How many times had she flung that phrase at Brand during the past two months? she wondered. He'd said, as far back as the day he'd questioned her about the tabloid photo of her and Chet Walker, that he knew she wasn't. But had he really meant it?

And did it matter? Whether he thought of her as a twenty-four-year-old girl or a twenty-four-year-old woman, he'd sent her away. He'd made love to her once and then he'd sent her away.

But why? It was a question she'd asked herself over and over.

Brand had wanted her. He's said so. She would have been willing to settle for that. She was still, to her shame, willing to settle for it. If Brand were to call her or to come to her right this very minute...

Cassie crossed her arms in front of her and hugged herself, trying not to cry. Her body ached. Her temples throbbed. A sense of frustration swept through her like a hot, dry wind.

Her lips shaped the single syllable that had become an instrument of torture for her.

Why?

Why had Brand sent her away?

Because she'd been a virgin?

Because she'd said she loved him?

Because she wasn't Sheila Parker?

Cassie squeezed her eyelids shut. She felt a tear trickle down her left cheek, then another trickle down her right.

"Oh, Brand," she murmured.

After a few moments, Cassie shook her head and opened her eyes once again. She swiped at her tear-dampened cheeks with the fingers of both hands, then undid her seat belt. After gathering her belongings, she got out of the car and shut the door. There was no need to slam it closed anymore. The locks now functioned like precision-crafted instruments. Her uncle had bowed to her wishes that he not buy her a new car for her birthday. Instead he'd spent a fortune having her old clunker overhauled inside and out.

There was no spring in her step as she walked toward the Marcus Moviemaking offices. Cassie realized this and felt a sudden spurt of anger at herself. She lifted her chin a notch, squared her shoulders and picked up her pace.

She reached the front door. She pulled it open. She marched into the lobby with her head held higher than it had been in nine days.

Then Cassie came to a dead stop, staring at the reception desk. Tina was sitting behind it. Noreen Krebs was standing to the right of it. A third woman was standing in front of it.

She was blond. She was beautiful. She was Brand Marcus's lover.

"Sheila," Cassie said numbly, "what are you doing in L.A.?"

A dozen different emotions sleeted across the actress's face. "I'm in L.A. for a doctor's appointment," she said. "But I'm here to see you."

Cassie blinked, her gaze darting from Sheila, to Tina, to Noreen, and back again. "A doctor's appointment?" she repeated, ignoring the second half of what the other woman had said. "Are you sick?"

"Only in the morning," Sheila answered, then smiled a smile that struck Cassie to the heart. "I'm pregnant."

Five minutes later, Cassie found herself sitting woozily on a low-slung leather sofa in Brand's office. She was watching Sheila Parker usher Noreen Krebs and half a dozen other Marcus Moviemaking staffers out the door. She had no clear recollection of how she'd gotten from the lobby to her present location.

She raised a shaky hand to a clammy brow. Pregnant. Sheila had said she was pregnant. Dear God. *That* she remembered.

"Well," the actress said, closing the door very firmly and turning around. "I wanted to surprise you with my news,

Cassie, but I never intended to make you faint. Even Graham's reaction wasn't that drastic."

"Graham knows?" How in the name of heaven could Sheila be so utterly callous? Cassie wondered, levering herself up off the sofa. How could she stand there beaming like the sun and acting as though she expected congratulations?

Sheila's smile faded. "Of course he knows," she said quietly, moving across the room to where Cassie was standing on none-too-steady feet. "He's the baby's father. Oh—" She grasped one of Cassie's arms. "Easy. Easy. That's it. Sit back down."

Cassie took a shaky breath. She stared up at the actress. "Graham?" she asked, not caring how desperate for reassurance she sounded.

"My husband, Graham," Sheila affirmed, then looked Cassie square in the eye. "You thought it was Brand's baby, didn't you?" she asked.

Cassie felt her cheeks flame for an instant, then grow pale. She made a helpless little gesture.

Sheila shook her head and sighed. "I was afraid it was something like this," she said obscurely. She reached into the right pocket of the cream silk blazer she was wearing. Her hand was clenched when she brought it out of the pocket. She extended her fist toward Cassie. "This is yours," she said, and let her fingers blossom open.

Sitting in the center of her palm was a gleaming gold whistle with the name "Cassie" engraved on it.

For several moments, Cassie stared at the birthday gift she'd discarded, then reclaimed it with trembling fingers. "W-where—?"

"I found it on the ground outside your room the night of your birthday party." Sheila sank gracefully onto the sofa. "You dropped it, didn't you? Or... threw it away?"

Cassie shrank from the images her mind began to replay inside her head. "I didn't want it anymore."

"Because you thought the man who'd given it to you had been unfaithful."

Cassie fingers tightened around the whistle. She glared at the other woman. "I *saw* you and Brand. I *heard* you."

Sheila shook her head. "It wasn't what you think."

Cassie made a bitterly skeptical sound.

The actress regarded her with a very strange expression. "Cassie, do you have that little confidence in your relationship with Brand?"

"My relationship—" Cassie nearly choked. She started to get up.

Sheila caught her arm. "You left Brand because you thought he was having an affair with me, didn't you?"

Horrified, Cassie jerked herself free. "Is that what he told you?"

"No, that's not what he told me!" The actress's melodious voice snapped like a whip. "Brand hasn't said a word to me—or anybody else—that hasn't had to do with *Prodigal* since you left."

There was a short, sharp silence. Cassie had gotten to her feet again, intending to leave the room. Yet there was something about the vehemence of the actress's last statement that made her go still.

Sheila looked up at her. "Cassie, I know what you saw and heard the night of your birthday upset you. And I'm sorry. I'm so, so sorry. But it wasn't what you think! Yes, Brand and I had an affair once. It was short and not very sweet. It had nothing—*nothing*—to do with love. To tell you the truth, I don't think we even liked each other very much while it was going on. That came afterward. We became friends."

"Friends," Cassie repeated neutrally.

"Yes, friends. Just friends. I swear to you. Then I met Graham and . . . oh." The actress's eyes suddenly took on a misty glow. "I never knew. I never knew I could feel about a man the way I feel about Graham. And so we got married. And there were problems in the beginning. I turned to Brand for advice. It was stupid, I realize. But I trusted him. Then Graham found out and he got jealous. I told him there was no reason. I told him over and over. But he didn't believe me. He didn't believe me until he saw you and Brand together."

Cassie slowly reseated herself on the sofa. "What about the night of my birthday party?"

Sheila sighed. "I never intended to get pregnant. It was a shock to discover I was going to have a baby. Then I realized I *wanted* to have a child. Graham's child. Only, well, Graham is twenty years older than I am. His age doesn't matter to me. But it matters to him. That was one of the problems we had when we first got married. And so I started to think about that and the idea of an unplanned baby and I began to worry. I had no idea how Graham would react if I told him he was going to become a father for the first time at age fifty-four. I didn't know what he might do. I was afraid I might lose him." Her expression became bleak for a few seconds as she contemplated this possibility.

The look of bleakness dissolved the last of Cassie's doubts. She knew that look too well. She'd seen it in her bathroom mirror that morning as she'd thought about her future without Brand. She tightened her grip on the gold whistle she still held nestled in her right palm.

"So," she concluded, "you told Brand you were pregnant and asked his advice."

The actress smiled just a little. "Actually he guessed."

Something clicked inside Cassie's head. "Morning sickness in makeup and crackers on the set!"

Sheila nodded, coloring slightly. "I've also been awfully weepy. I started crying when I was in the room with Brand. He gave me a hug, Cassie. And then he told me to go find my husband and tell him the truth. Which I finally did two days ago."

"And?"

"And Graham was ecstatic." The actress smiled dreamily for a few moments, then grew serious. "You do believe me, don't you?" she asked anxiously. "About Brand and me? About what you heard and saw?"

Cassie nodded once.

"In that case, will you come back to Texas?"

Cassie glanced away for a second. The knowledge that Brand had not lied to her about his relationship with Sheila eased some of the pain she'd been feeling. But it could not salve the true source of her heartache. "I can't," she said in a small voice.

"What do you mean, you can't?" Sheila sounded surprised and upset. "Cassie, you have to! You just told me you believe—"

Cassie looked back at the other woman. "I didn't leave because I thought you and Brand were having an affair."

The actress grimaced. "Oh, please, don't try to tell me it was because of your uncle's car accident. I've already heard the story about the deal he closed on the pay phone in the emergency room."

Cassie swallowed. "I didn't want to go," she said starkly. "Brand sent me away."

Sheila's eyes went wide and her brows shot halfway to her hairline. "What?"

Cassie repeated herself.

"Sent you away? The man loves you!"

Cassie flinched. "No, he doesn't."

"Of course, he does! My God, Cassie. He married you."

"Sheila—"

"Oh, I know it was under strange circumstances. To tell you the truth, I'm still trying to figure out what happened. At first Graham thought it was a shotgun wedding with your uncle carrying the shotgun. I mean, it's no secret that Jordan comes on like a Victorian papa where you're concerned. But Graham said later the look on Brand's face when he watched you come down the chapel aisle convinced him it was no put-up job. Besides, when you consider the way he and I rushed to the altar, your elopement to Las Vegas was pretty tame."

"Sheila—" Cassie tried to interrupt again.

"And beyond the fact that Brand married you," the actress continued, "there's the way he's been acting since you left."

"That's just it, Sheila!" Cassie cried. "It's *acting*! It's all been acting!"

The actress stared at her blankly. "Acting?"

"We made believe. We pretended. We lied."

Sheila shook her head. "I don't understand, Cassie."

Cassie hesitated, considering everything that had gone before. At the very least she owed Sheila Parker the truth, she thought.

She took a deep breath, then said very deliberately, "It all began with *Prodigal*..."

The story obviously left Sheila Parker stunned.

"My God," she whispered when Cassie finally stopped speaking about fifteen minutes later.

Cassie brushed a lock of hair back behind her ear. "Now do you see why I can't go back to Texas?" she asked wearily. Recounting the events of the past two months had been a draining experience.

The actress remained silent for several seconds. It was almost as though she hadn't heard the question. Then with surprising conviction, she declared, "No, I don't."

Cassie had started to slump back against the sofa. Her spine stiffened at Sheila's tone.

"What I see," the other woman went on inexorably, "is two people who should be together but who aren't. I see two people who are very much in love."

"Brand isn't in love with me, Sheila!" Cassie protested rawly.

There was compassion in the actress's eyes. There was a hint of exasperation, as well. "Do you have any idea what's been going on in Texas since you left?" she asked.

Cassie shook her head. "Not really," she conceded. The first few days she'd been back, she'd been thankful to remain ignorant. To be reminded of what she'd left behind in any way had been just too painful. But that had changed. The need to know had begun to gnaw at her. "I've heard filming's going better than expected."

Sheila smiled crookedly. "That depends on what you expected. Yes, the dailies look incredible. And yes, we're ahead of schedule." Her smile vanished and her expression turned grim. "But Brand is killing himself by inches, Cassie, and he's inflicting a lot of damage on other people while he's doing it."

Cassie went cold. "What?"

"He's not eating. He's not sleeping. He's working like a madman. He's driven most of the crew to the brink of quitting."

"Brand?"

"Yes, Brand. He's had shouting matches with at least a dozen different people during the past nine days. Including Graham. He's falling apart, Cassie, and he doesn't seem to care. Now I don't pretend to understand everything that's happened between the two of you. But I've seen Brand with you and I've seen Brand without you. And whatever his reasons were for sending you away, they didn't include not loving you."

Cassie looked away from the other woman and down at her right hand. She unclenched her fingers and stared at the whistle Brand had given her, trying to reconcile what Sheila was saying with what she believed to be true.

"Did you tell Brand you found this?" she asked.

"No. And I didn't tell him I was coming here to see you, either."

Cassie lifted her eyes. "He never said he loved me."

"I realize that."

"If he loves me, wouldn't he want me to know?"

"Not if he's afraid you don't feel the same way."

"I told him how I feel!"

"Tell him again."

Cassie said nothing for nearly thirty seconds. Finally she opened her mouth to speak, but was forestalled by a knock at the office door. She turned. So did Sheila.

The door opened. Noreen Krebs stuck her head in. She was wearing an anxious expression. "Is everything all right?" she asked.

Cassie wasn't conscious of making a decision. She simply went from a state of confusion to one of absolute certainty in the space of a single heartbeat. "I need to know when the next plane for Texas leaves, Noreen," she announced. She heard Sheila catch her breath.

Noreen's eyes narrowed. "Why?"

There were a thousand and one ways Cassie could have answered this, including telling the older woman to mind her own business. Instead she told the absolute truth. "Because my husband's there."

Noreen Krebs was not, by any stretch of the imagination, a beautiful woman. But the smile that blossomed on her face made her seem so. "There's a flight in ninety minutes."

"That doesn't give you any time to pack," Sheila said.

"So?" Cassie laughed and got to her feet. She felt as though she were floating. "Noreen—"

"I've already made a first-class reservation in your name," Noreen interrupted. She opened the door wider and held out a package. "And I got this out of your office. I still don't suppose a pure silk peignoir set is the most practical thing to take on a location shoot, but, well, maybe you'll find a use for it."

Chapter Fifteen

Dusk was falling when Cassie let herself into room 114 of the Bide-a-While Motel. Her fingers shook a bit as she worked the lock on the door. She was aware that her heart was beating much more quickly than normal.

She did not expect to find Brand inside. She knew he was shooting a sundown sequence at a location about an hour away. She'd gleaned this information from Bobby Ray Delbert, who'd been waiting at the tiny local airport when she'd deplaned roughly forty-five minutes before. His presence had surprised her. He'd been quick to explain that he'd been dispatched by Lee Allen in response to an imperative phone call from Noreen Krebs.

He'd also been extremely eager to apologize for his behavior the night of her birthday party. Behavior that, she'd gathered, he only dimly remembered.

"I didn't mean for you to fall into the pool," he'd told her with great sincerity, his eyes ping-ponging back and forth between the road and her face. "And I sure didn't mean to cause any trouble between you and your husband. I mean, when I found out you'd up and left the next morning—"

"It's all right, Bobby," she'd assured him firmly. "Really. It's all right." And if it's not, she'd amended silently, it's going to be.

Cassie stepped inside the motel room and closed the door behind her. She stood for just a moment, listening to the hum of the air-conditioning unit. Then she flicked on the light switch by the door.

Memories of the last time she'd been in this room came flooding back. She's spent a miserable week and a half trying to escape these memories. Now she accepted them, embraced them. She had a new perspective on what had happened between her and Brand in this room, thanks to Sheila Parker.

Gradually the rushing tide of memories ebbed and Cassie came back to the present. She glanced around. There was something different about the room. Something she couldn't quite put her finger on.

And then she knew. The towel hanging from the knob of the connecting door. The jeans and shirt carelessly tossed to the end of the bed. The stack of storyboards piled in one corner. They could only mean one thing.

Brand had been living in this room. In *her* room.

Cassie felt her heart skip a beat. Brand could have remained in the adjoining room, she realized. But, no. He'd moved in here. He'd chosen to stay where she'd stayed. Sleep where she'd slept.

Her gaze returned to the bed. She trembled a little, remembering.

She and Brand. *Together.*

Kissing. Caressing.

Intimate.

Erotic.

Utterly, absolutely, right.

After a few seconds, Cassie walked toward the bed, coming to a halt at the end of it. She picked up the discarded shirt and stroked it with fingers that weren't quite steady. She let herself imagine it was Brand she was stroking. Her eyelids fluttered down and she recalled something Sheila Parker had said just before they'd gone their separate ways that morning.

"Sometimes men don't say the words, Cassie," the actress had declared with a very womanly kind of ruefulness. "Sometimes they expect us to figure it out for ourselves. And they get very angry when we don't. I mean, their feelings are so obvious to them, they can't understand why they aren't obvious to us."

Cassie's memory played back a series vignettes involving Brand.

You seem to have a talent for remaining oblivious to the obvious in some situations, he'd told her on one occasion.

Dammit, Cassie, there are a lot of things you don't notice! he'd practically shouted at her on another.

And then, the night they'd made love.

Me? she'd flung at him. *You want to know what's wrong with me? Why don't you figure out what's wrong with you?*

I don't have to figure it out. I already know. You're what's wrong with me.

"No, Brand," Cassie whispered. "I'm what's right with you."

Every second... of every minute... of every hour... of every day, he'd gone on. *It's hell being with you. It's hell being without you.*

Cassie opened her eyes. That had hardly been the most romantic confession of love in history, she reflected. But every instinct she had now told her it was one of the most real.

"Oh, Brand," she said aloud, her gaze straying around the room. "Oh—"

She stopped, focusing on something lying on top of the small nightstand to the right of the bed. It was a snapshot.

Cassie let Brand's shirt fall from her fingers. She took two steps forward and picked up the picture. Her vision blurred briefly, but it didn't matter. She knew what the snapshot showed.

She knew because of Eula Mae Bertram. She'd seen the woman about ten minutes before when she'd gone into the registration office of the Bide-a-While Motel to get the key to room 114.

"So you came back," Eula Mae had said, scratching her nose.

"Yes, Miss Bertram, I've come back," she'd replied.

"Kinda thought you would."

"Did you?"

"Yeah." Eula Mae had continued scratching. "I get feelin's about some things sometimes. I'm real good at predictin' tornadoes. Course, this time, I didn't need any twinges in my back to tell me how things were going to be. I saw that picture from your party and I knew."

"Picture? What picture?"

The proprietress of the Bide-a-While Motel had smiled at this point. "Ask your husband. It's his now."

Cassie blinked against the tears that were filming her eyes and stared down at the photograph she was holding. It was the one Eula Mae Bertram had taken just moments after she'd opened Brand's birthday present. The two of them were gazing at each other as though they were the only people in the world.

If you want me, just whistle.

Lauren Bacall to Humphrey Bogart.

Cassie Addams to Brand Marcus.

Brand Marcus to . . . his wife.

Cassie smiled. She hoped what she had in mind would be more effective than whistling.

Brand came back to the room roughly three hours later. Cassie was drowsing and daydreaming on the bed they'd once shared when she heard the sound of gravel being crunched underfoot outside the door. She sat up abruptly, her heart pounding, her mouth dry. The nearly euphoric confidence that had buoyed her since that morning was replaced by a wild sense of anxiety.

The rattle of a key being placed in a lock and turned.

Cassie had asked Bobby Ray Delbert not to say anything about her return. He'd told her that Lee Allan had already instructed him that it was a surprise and had solemnly sworn to remain silent about her presence.

The click of a lock giving way.

It was possible, she knew, that Eula Mae Bertram might have told Brand what was waiting for him in room 114. But somehow she didn't think the motel owner would do that.

The creak of a hinge that needed oiling.

Cassie swung her legs off the bed and stood. Her long, loose hair shifted around her shoulders. The sleek silk nightgown and robe she was wearing rippled against her body. She pressed her right hand, the hand that was clutching a precious gold whistle, to her breast.

The door opened.

Cassie bit her lip to keep from crying out Brand's name and her love.

He had not expected to see her. Not here. Not tonight. That much was starkly evident from the way he stilled and stiffened. Only that morning, Cassie might have read rejection in the sudden rigidity of Brand's body, but not now. She saw what was in his face, understood what was in his heart.

Brand Marcus looked like a man who had just had his dearest, most desperately held wish granted. His blue eyes blazed with a joy that was unguarded and absolute.

Whatever fears Cassie had been harboring vanished. They did not return even when she saw Brand's expression turn hard and shuttered. She finally knew what he was trying to hide and why.

"What are you doing here?" he asked.

Cassie heard the hope beneath the harshness of this question. She lifted her chin a little and brushed at her hair with her left hand. She saw Brand's eyes follow the movement and knew, to the instant, when he registered the fa she was still wearing his rings.

Brand took a step forward, then stopped himself fro going any farther with a visible effort. "What are you doin here?" he repeated.

His dark hair was untidy and needed a trim. His face wa thinner than she remembered and there were new lines c stress etched into the skin at the corners of his eyes an mouth. His clothes looked as though he'd slept i them . . . assuming he'd slept at all since he'd put them on.

Oh, Brand, Cassie thought. Oh, Brand, why did we d this to each other? We could have been sharing heaven th past nine days. Instead we've been living in separate hells.

"Cassie?" Brand took another step forward, a disquie ing emotion flickering across his face. Cassie realized he wa beginning to fear that what he was seeing wasn't real.

She wet her lips with a quick lick of her tongue, then f nally spoke. "What I'm doing here is waiting for you," sh answered.

"No." He shook his head. Cassie understood that Bran was denying the possibility because he didn't dare let hin self believe it.

"Yes," she countered softly.

He flinched as though she'd struck him. "Why?"

Cassie smiled at him, knowing her heart was in her eye "Because I love you."

"Cassie—"

"And because you love me, Brand. You love me as muc as I love you."

"You don't—"

"Know what I'm saying? Yes, I do. I love you. And yo love—"

She broke off with a gasp as Brand closed the distanc between them and pulled her close against him. "No," h said in a low, unsteady voice. "Let me say it. Let me finall say it." His arms tightened around her. "I love you, Cas sie. I love you . . . I love you . . . I love you."

He sought and found her mouth then, kissing her as though he were a man dying of hunger and she was a banquet. His lips moved over hers with devouring, undisguised need. Cassie gloried in the feel of it.

"Oh, Cassie...oh, love. Sweet...you don't know..." he murmured disjointedly, marking the features of her face with kisses.

She brought her arms up around his neck, weaving her fingers deep into his dark hair. "Yes," she responded. "Yes, I do."

"Oh, Cassie," Brand groaned. One of his hands swept up her spine to cup the back of her head.

Cassie went up on tiptoe. "Make love with me, Brand," she half pleaded, half demanded. "Make love with me... now."

He did.

An ecstatic eternity later, Cassie lay nestled in the curve of Brand's arm, her cheek resting on the place above his heart. She was deliciously aware of the slow drift of his fingers over her body.

"I have a question," he said quietly.

Cassie turned her head a little, the silken spill of her bright hair shifting against his leanly muscled chest. "Only one?" she teased, then caught her breath as his exploratory caresses became intimate. "Mmm..." she sighed blissfully. "Ask me anything."

He chuckled. "Where did you get what you were wearing earlier?"

Cassie blinked. The press of Brand's flesh against hers made it difficult to contemplate ever having worn anything. Then she remembered. "Oh. Noreen gave it to me."

"Noreen?"

She lifted her head so she could look at him. "You said she was a romantic."

His mouth quirked. "I think I underestimated her."

"You liked it?"

"Truth?"

"Of course."

"Better off than on."

Cassie laughed a little and kissed the ridge of his coll bone.

"She called me a damned fool, you know," he observ after a few moments.

"Noreen?"

"Mmm."

"When?"

"Yesterday."

Cassie had been brushing her fingertips against the da springy hair on his chest. She paused and looked at hi "You spoke to her?"

He stroked one hand down her back. "Every day sir you went away. I needed to know that you were all right.

"I wasn't."

"So Noreen told me." He paused. "I was anything but right, too."

Cassie dipped her head and brushed her lips against skin. "So Sheila Parker told me," she admitted.

"Sheila?"

She nodded. Then, because she knew it was necessary, s related her conversation with the woman who had once be his lover, but not his love.

"I owe Sheila a great deal," Brand said when she fi ished.

"We both do," Cassie returned.

There was a brief silence. Brand shifted suddenly, a Cassie felt a hint of tension enter his body. She thought s knew why. A moment later, her suspicion was confirmed

"We need to talk about what happened the night of yo birthday party," he said. "What I did—"

"What *we* both did," she corrected.

Brand eased away from her, propping himself up on o elbow. He shook his head, his eyes shadowed. "Cassie, y were a virgin. I feel—"

"Guilty? Is that why you sent me away?"

His throat worked. "Yes."

"Why should you feel guilty? Because you gave me pleasure? You did, you know, Brand. I...I had no idea making love could be like that."

He flushed slightly, a hint of boyishness tempering the grave maturity of his expression. "Neither did I," he said huskily. "But—"

"Do you wish you hadn't been the first man who made love to me?" she pressed. "Do you wish those things you believed about me and Chet Walker and who knows how many others had been true?"

"God, no!" Brand answered. "Dear God, no."

"Well, then? I'm glad there wasn't anyone before you, Brand. Do you hear me? I'm glad."

He cupped her cheek in his palm. "I can't pretend there weren't others before you, Cassie."

"I don't want you to. I don't want you to pretend anything anymore."

"I never felt for any of them what I feel for you. I never knew I was capable of feeling what I feel for you. I love you so much."

"And I love you."

They kissed and caressed for several minutes. Cassie blossomed in response to Brand's tender, nurturing touch. She moved against him languorously, savoring the sweet heat her husband was stirring within her.

"Did you really believe I'd been with Chet Walker?" she asked eventually.

Brand grimaced a little and stroked a lock of hair back from her face. "I don't know what I really believed," he confessed with a sigh. "I was jealous, Cassie. I was jealous of Chet and Lee Allen and every other man you looked at or smiled or talked to. It killed me to see you paying attention to them when you were so oblivious to me."

Cassie laughed. She couldn't help it. "Oblivious? Oh, Brand! If only you knew."

He shifted, obviously not offended by her laughter. She saw a glint of self-mockery in his eyes. "Well, why don't you fill me—ouch! What the—" Twisting, he reached underneath himself.

"My whistle!" Cassie exclaimed when she saw what was in his hand. She took it from him. "You never told me what this was supposed to mean," she said, flashing him a flirtatious smile.

Brand took the small gold object back and set it on the bedside table along with the snapshot Eula Mae Bertram had taken. "If you don't know what it means by now, sweetheart, my explanation isn't going to help."

Cassie sensed that he used the endearment deliberately. A delicious little quiver ran through her. "Were you *really* jealous?" she inquired.

His sensuallly shaped mouth twisted. "Yes, I was really jealous. I think everyone in the world knew that but you. Including your uncle."

"Uncle Jordan?"

"Mmm. I've always had a feeling that's one of the main reasons he kept calling me to discuss how worried he was about you."

It took Cassie a few moments to unravel this comment. "Oh," she said on a quick intake of breath. "You think he was..." Her voice trailed off.

No, she thought. It couldn't be. Her uncle was a die-hard practitioner of the fine art of manipulating other people for their own good, but not even *he* could have behaved so deviously.

"Do I think he was fanning the flames?" Brand picked up with a slightly exasperated chuckle. "Well, let's just say I wouldn't put it past him."

Cassie sat up. After a moment, Brand did, too. She regarded him steadily. "Did you tell my uncle you were in love with me?" she asked.

He stroked her hair back behind her ears. "No, I didn't."

"But you did tell him any intentions you had toward me were honorable."

He let his hands slide to her naked shoulders, then began stroking them down her arms. "Cassie, you've been someone special to me since you first came to Marcus Moviemaking. I didn't realize how special until the day I hired you as my personal assistant. I fell in love with you that day, but it took me a while to realize it. When your uncle came to me about the rumor we were sleeping together, *I* was angrier about it than he was. I mean, I wanted you. I wanted you so badly I ached with it. That's one of the reasons I made sure you had your own office. I didn't trust myself to have you within reach all day every day. That's also one of the reasons I kept blowing up at you."

"You were trying to protect me from yourself."

He nodded.

"But why?"

Brand's eyes grew tender. "Because you were young and vulnerable and I was afraid I'd hurt you. Because I knew, no matter what you were doing with Chet Walker or anybody else, you were an innocent compared with me. Because I didn't understand what loving a woman really meant. And selfishly, because you're the best assistant I've ever had and I didn't want to lose you."

"Oh, Brand..."

"At the same time," he went on, "I realized that even if I did find a way to handle being your boss and your lover, it wouldn't be enough. I wanted more. Just how much more, I didn't know. Or if I did, I wouldn't admit it to myself. Still, that's why I told your uncle my intentions were honorable. It wasn't so much a promise to him as a pledge to myself."

Brand grasped her hands with his at this point and raised the right, then the left, to his lips. "I don't know how much of Jordan's performance the day we got married was put-on and how much was genuine. I do know that he thinks of you as his daughter, Cassie. And I think it's hard for a father, even a father with matchmaking on his mind, to come face-to-face with what looks like proof that his little girl has grown up in every sense of the word."

Cassie felt her cheeks grow warm and she remembered how passionately she'd wished what her uncle had thought had been true. "Matchmaking?" she wondered aloud, repeating the word Brand had used. "My uncle?"

Brand kissed her hands again. "We'll never know for sure, Cassie. But now that we're truly together, he'll probably take credit for it."

Cassie nodded her agreement. "There is one more thing," she said slowly. "What about the plan to deceive Graham? Was that all because of *Prodigal*?"

Brand drew her closer. "The film means a lot to me. But you mean much, much more. What I told you about my reasons for proposing the scheme was the truth. It just wasn't the whole truth. Deep down, I hoped what we were pretending would become real."

Cassie smiled, knowing she'd hoped the same thing. "It has, Brand. Oh, it has."

"I love you."

"I love you, too."

A long time later.

"Brand?"

"Yes, sweetheart?"

"This is much better than make-believe."

"I was just thinking the same thing."

* * * * *

PASSPORT TO ROMANCE VACATION SWEEPSTAKES

OFFICIAL RULES

SWEEPSTAKES RULES AND REGULATIONS. NO PURCHASE NECESSARY.

HOW TO ENTER:

1. To enter, complete this official entry form and return with your invoice in the envelope provided, or print your name, address, telephone number and age on a plain piece of paper and mail to: Passport to Romance, P.O. Box #1397, Buffalo, N.Y. 14269-1397. No mechanically reproduced entries accepted.
2. All entries must be received by the Contest Closing Date, midnight, December 31, 1990 to be eligible.
3. Prizes: There will be ten (10) Grand Prizes awarded, each consisting of a choice of a trip for two people to: i) London, England (approximate retail value $5,050 U.S.); ii) England, Wales and Scotland (approximate retail value $6,400 U.S.); iii) Caribbean Cruise (approximate retail value $7,300 U.S.); iv) Hawaii (approximate retail value $ 9,550 U.S.); v) Greek Island Cruise in the Mediterranean (approximate retail value $12,250 U.S.); vi) France (approximate retail value $7,300 U.S.).
4. Any winner may choose to receive any trip or a cash alternative prize of $5,000.00 U.S. in lieu of the trip.
5. Odds of winning depend on number of entries received.
6. A random draw will be made by Nielsen Promotion Services, an independent judging organization on January 29, 1991, in Buffalo, N.Y , at 11:30 a.m. from all eligible entries received on or before the Contest Closing Date. Any Canadian entrants who are selected must correctly answer a time-limited, mathematical skill-testing question in order to win. Quebec residents may submit any litigation respecting the conduct and awarding of a prize in this contest to the Régie des loteries et courses du Quebec.
7. Full contest rules may be obtained by sending a stamped, self-addressed envelope to: "Passport to Romance Rules Request", P.O. Box 9998, Saint John, New Brunswick, E2L 4N4.
8. Payment of taxes other than air and hotel taxes is the sole responsibility of the winner.
9. Void where prohibited by law.

PASSPORT TO ROMANCE VACATION SWEEPSTAKES

OFFICIAL RULES

SWEEPSTAKES RULES AND REGULATIONS. NO PURCHASE NECESSARY.

HOW TO ENTER:

1. To enter, complete this official entry form and return with your invoice in the envelope provided, or print your name, address, telephone number and age on a plain piece of paper and mail to: Passport to Romance, P.O. Box #1397, Buffalo, N.Y. 14269-1397 No mechanically reproduced entries accepted.
2. All entries must be received by the Contest Closing Date, midnight, December 31, 1990 to be eligible.
3. Prizes: There will be ten (10) Grand Prizes awarded, each consisting of a choice of a trip for two people to: i) London, England (approximate retail value $5,050 U.S.); ii) England, Wales and Scotland (approximate retail value $6,400 U.S.); iii) Caribbean Cruise (approximate retail value $7,300 U.S.); iv) Hawaii (approximate retail value $ 9,550 U.S.); v) Greek Island Cruise in the Mediterranean (approximate retail value $12,250 U.S.); vi) France (approximate retail value $7,300 U.S.).
4. Any winner may choose to receive any trip or a cash alternative prize of $5,000.00 U.S. in lieu of the trip.
5. Odds of winning depend on number of entries received.
6. A random draw will be made by Nielsen Promotion Services, an independent judging organization on January 29, 1991, in Buffalo, N.Y., at 11:30 a.m. from all eligible entries received on or before the Contest Closing Date. Any Canadian entrants who are selected must correctly answer a time-limited, mathematical skill-testing question in order to win. Quebec residents may submit any litigation respecting the conduct and awarding of a prize in this contest to the Régie des loteries et courses du Quebec.
7. Full contest rules may be obtained by sending a stamped, self-addressed envelope to: "Passport to Romance Rules Request", P.O. Box 9998, Saint John, New Brunswick, E2L 4N4
8. Payment of taxes other than air and hotel taxes is the sole responsibility of the winner
9. Void where prohibited by law.

RLS-DIR

PASSPORT
WIN
1 of 10 Vacations
SEE INSIDE
TO ROMANCE

VACATION SWEEPSTAKES

MONTH 2 ENTRY

Official Entry Form

Yes, enter me in the drawing for one of ten Vacations-for-Two! If I'm a winner, I'll get my choice of any of the six different destinations being offered — and I won't have to decide until after I'm notified!

Return entries with invoice in envelope provided along with Daily Travel Allowance Voucher. Each book in your shipment has two entry forms — and the more you enter, the better your chance of winning!

Name ______________________________

Address ______________________ Apt. ______

City ____________ State/Prov. ____________ Zip/Postal Code ____________

Daytime phone number ______________________
Area Code

☐ I am enclosing a Daily Travel Allowance Voucher in the amount of $__________ Write in amount revealed beneath scratch-off

VACATION SWEEPSTAKES

MONTH 2 ENTRY

Official Entry Form

Yes, enter me in the drawing for one of ten Vacations-for-Two! If I'm a winner, I'll get my choice of any of the six different destinations being offered — and I won't have to decide until after I'm notified!

Return entries with invoice in envelope provided along with Daily Travel Allowance Voucher. Each book in your shipment has two entry forms — and the more you enter, the better your chance of winning!

Name ______________________________

Address ______________________ Apt. ______

City ____________ State/Prov. ____________ Zip/Postal Code ____________

Daytime phone number ______________________
Area Code

☐ I am enclosing a Daily Travel Allowance Voucher in the amount of $__________ Write in amount revealed beneath scratch-off

CPS-TWO